Food Trucks of the Zombie Apocalypse

HOPE SERVED HOT WITH A SIDE OF SMALL-TOWN ROMANCE

END TIMES COUNTRY BUFFET SERIES

BOOK ONE

DELILAH COOKE

CHAPTER 1
Whispering Skies

The sizzle of onions hitting the flattop griddle sliced through the late-morning air, staccato-like. Hawthorne Porter moved with the rhythm of an experienced short-order cook, grabbing, flipping, and plating orders in precision that stood out among the chaos crammed into the compact space of The Gourmet Grinder food truck.

"Extra pickles on that Reuben, Hawthorne," Frank barked, not looking up from his phone. "And toast the rye longer this time. We're not known for soggy bread. Not on my truck."

"You're not the cook," she muttered under her breath.

Rucha heard it and snorted from the service window, where she was wrestling with a crowd of underfed and overworked grad students ordering the cheapest sandwich on the menu and crying about their research. "You're testy today. Didn't Marla text you those affirmations again?"

"She did." Hawthorne flipped the sandwich, warm rye lifting off the griddle in a perfect arc. "Something about 'aligning your cheese with the stars,' but we started the day low on smoked paprika and now Frank is breathing down my neck with the enthusiasm of a poodle in heat."

Frank, naturally, didn't hear or chose not to care, his attention now rerouted to the tiny label printer on the counter next to Rucha, which had so far that day not fucked up even once. A miracle, in Hawthorne's opinion, and she hoped Frank wouldn't ruin the streak by poking at the machine.

"If you'd filed the supply order properly, we wouldn't be out of smoked paprika," Frank said, abandoning the printer to loom closer, his smile thin and performative. "Details matter, Hawthorne. That's what separates a real business from a food truck that dies in its first year."

"We've been open nearly two years," Rucha said pointedly, "and we're in the black."

"Exactly," Frank huffed with pride, as if he had any role in making the sandwich truck a success. "See? Patel knows what I'm talkin' about!"

But Hawthorne didn't respond, since she knew she'd never get any recognition out of him. The supply order had been filled out properly, but Frank had submitted it to their supplier a day too late for it to make it into their usual weekly delivery. Even if she pointed that out, he'd find a way to blame her, because that was just the kind of boss he was.

She was measuring red cabbage into paper cartons, steam rising with the vinegary tang of house-made slaw. Behind her, the line outside The Gourmet Grinder stretched down the sidewalk of the Calloway-Hayden A&M quad, mostly students mingling with professors and a few local townies who had caught on that this particular food truck made a killer barbecue tofu wrap. The background buzz of the crowd was familiar and comforting, the soundtrack of Hawthorne's life since she had dropped out of college to help her mother take care of her dying father five years ago. It mixed with the scent of flowering crepe myrtles and the first sign of spring humidity, settling in her chest with a hint nostalgia. It had been her father's favorite time of year.

Rucha had turned the little pass-through beside the service window into command central, weaving between orders with a cool efficiency Hawthorne admired. Rucha was all business under her bright yellow bandana and perfectly applied eyeliner, calling out names with the patience of a preschool teacher and the authority of a seasoned air traffic controller.

"Benny with the Americano and no-egg breakfast wrap!" she called, placing the steaming drink and foil-wrapped bundle on the window ledge. She leaned out, scanning the eager faces. "No substitutions next time, Benny. You're rubbing Frank's chi the wrong way."

"Hey!" Benny grinned, grabbing his order. "Tell Frank I'm workshopping jokes for open mic night. He inspires me."

Rucha raised a brow and turned back toward the espresso machine. "You hear that, Frank? You're a muse for the theater kids."

Frank, furiously trying to unjam the label printer like it had insulted his honor, just made a strangled noise.

"Oh, here's your problem," Rucha said sweetly, pulling the flap open with an audible click and tugging out the offending sticky strips. "You keep ordering the off-brand labels."

"It's not the labels," Frank said defensively.

"It's always the labels," Hawthorne chimed, not looking up from the griddle.

If her timing was right—and it was always right—the spicy jackfruit melt needed flipping. A flick of her wrist, and each edge caramelized like a dream, the curl of savory smoke twisting upward. For a moment, the scent banished the world of bad bosses and missed opportunities. It was a small, golden thing, just a tiny bite of satisfaction in a too-small space, but it mattered to her.

"Pickup for Anika!" Rucha called, glancing over at her. "Did you do the aioli?"

Hawthorne nodded. "Garlic lemon, extra on the side like she likes."

"Because you're a treasure." Rucha smiled benevolently as she pushed the carton forward.

Anika, a familiar regular customer, took her lunch and flashed a grateful smile, then paused. "Y'all hear about the gas shortage? My roommate went to fuel up last night and said half the pumps are closed."

Hawthorne perked up. "That's weird. Fairhope's got at least three delivery routes through here now."

Anika shrugged, halfway through biting her wrap. "Yeah, I dunno. Add it to the list—weird power outages, missing buses, and they canceled afternoon classes in Carver Hall."

"Wait! Classes in Carver are cancelled?" Someone in the line perked up at the news.

"It's here! Fire in the veins of the earth, and death walks on sticky feet!"

From somewhere beyond the quad, a voice like gravel rose into the air.

Heads turned, and Rucha froze with a lid halfway closed over the iced lemonade she was prepping. "Oh boy," she said softly, glancing toward the edge of the crowd near the big magnolia tree.

Hawthorne didn't even have to look. "Twister?"

"Twister," Rucha confirmed, setting the cup down and pressing a finger to her temple. "Hope she's not doing the plagues-of-Egypt today. I forgot my allergy meds."

As if summoned by their comments, the tall, wiry figure of Twister emerged from the sidewalk shadows. Wrapped in layers that defied both temperature and logic—two coats (one with a broken zipper), a threadbare Hello Kitty scarf, combat boots with neon duct tape wrapped around the toes—she moved across the pathway with the theatrical flair of someone on a mission too divine for earthly concerns.

She waved a crooked broomstick like a warning flag, tufts of faded pink feathers tied to the end fluttering in the breeze. Her white hair stuck out under a wide-brimmed straw hat covered in bottle caps and handwritten signs: "DO NOT TRUST THE FROGS" and "ASK ME ABOUT THE END TIMES PANINI."

Students parted around her like water. No one dared try to stop her. Twister had been a known feature of Fairhope for longer than anyone could remember. Some said she used to be a professor. Others swore she once lived in the fire tower out in the state park, taming hawks and reading tea leaves. Hawthorne wasn't sure if any of it was true, but she liked to think it was all a little bit true. That was the kind of story Twister seemed to walk out of, anyway.

"THE SKY'S BEEN WHISPERIN'," Twister howled toward the library steps. "AND THE BIRDS? THEY KNOW. OH, THEY KNOW."

"She's really going for it today," Rucha murmured, stealing a glance.

Frank stormed up beside them, arms crossed rigidly. "Someone call campus security. She's gonna scare off our lunch rush."

"Frank," Rucha said, tone level but warning, "it's Twister. She's like campus furniture. You don't ask the mossy statue to stop making people nervous."

"She's doing performance art or spreading a prophecy, and either way, it's Fairhope. Let her cook," Hawthorne said, sliding a tray of crispy hash patties onto the warmer with a flourish. "Besides, she's not hurting anyone. Unless she starts tossing frogs. That happened once."

"They weren't actual frogs," Rucha murmured, eyes still on Twister as she paused dramatically mid-quad, broomstick rooted to the bricks like it had taken divine revelation to the shin. "It was a bunch of squeezy stress balls she fished out of the trash."

"Meh. Same difference," Hawthorne said with a shrug.

Twister tilted her head skyward, arms raised like she was waiting for a lightning bolt, or maybe a pigeon with aggressive opinions. A hush spread across the quad; even the griddle seemed to drop in temperature, causing Hawthorne to curse at it.

"YOU THINK IT'S JUST A RUMBLE IN THE PIPES," she declared, twirling once, coat flaring like a cape. "BUT IT'S THE WEIGHING OF THE HEARTS! THE WORMS KNOW WHAT'S COMING."

That earned a quiet ripple of appreciative murmurs from Benny and the knot of theater students sitting under a tulip poplar. One of them started slow-clapping. Another took out their phone to start streaming or recording, probably. Twister had a small online following among the undergrads, who thought she was doing some avant-garde interactive fiction thing. Hawthorne suspected half of them hoped she was part of the writing department's immersive storytelling lab.

"She's gonna end up on TikTok again," Rucha deadpanned, finally finishing the lemonade and handing it off. "I still can't believe that 'kumquats are the devil's eggs' video got fifty thousand likes."

"She was right about the spinach recall last year," Hawthorne noted, leaning on her elbow for a moment between tickets. "Maybe she's just tuned into a weird frequency the rest of us can't hear."

Frank gave them a withering look that was probably meant to be intimidating but landed somewhere around constipated possum. "She's a public nuisance. What she needs is a clean shirt and a welfare check."

"What she needs is some respect," Rucha shot back, brows knitting together. "She's part of this town, whether you like it or not. Probably more than you."

"Exactly." Hawthorne smirked. "Besides, you scare off more customers than she does. With your... whole 'clipboard gladiator' energy."

Frank's face swelled like a boiled sausage, but then he got distracted again by the label printer beeping at him forlornly. Hawthorne took the moment to swipe a tofu wrap that Frank had said was "done wrong" and set aside to toss later (or eat for himself, more likely).

"Pee run!" She ducked out of the back door while Frank squawked in outrage that she had not asked permission first. Hawthorne didn't actually need to pee. She just needed fresh air in her lungs and a moment away from the endless hiss of the griddle and Frank's eternal crusade against joy.

She looped around to the alley that ran beside the Chemistry Annex, the side of campus where old brick met older brick and not much ever happened, except for the occasional visiting German scientist who smoked cigarettes by the dumpster.

Twister was leaning against the outside bulletin board, poking at the pockmarked cork with her broomstick. When she heard Hawthorne's footsteps, she stilled. Her hat shifted slightly, the bottle caps tinkling like little tin wind chimes in the sunlight that had started to bleed through the clouds.

"I told them," she said without turning around, her voice unexpectedly calm. "Told 'em about the worms and the frogs and the whisperin' fire and the pulsing in the soil. But they make jokes. They always do."

"I brought you a sandwich," Hawthorne replied, quietly.

Twister turned slowly, without drama, as though she only had so many rotations left in her. Up close, her eyes were startlingly clear beneath their grime and crinkles. Blue and sharp, like thin ice waiting to break free.

"I knew you would," Twister said, cradling the sandwich like it was wrapped in gold. "This one," she added, nodding toward Hawthorne, "has good kitchen bones."

"I, uh... thanks?" Hawthorne smiled, unsure whether that was a compliment or some kind of culinary haunting.

Twister peeled back the foil slowly, reverently. She sniffed the onions, the tofu, the slaw, as if communing with ingredients on a spiritual plane, and then tore a hunk off and shoved it into her mouth with surprising gusto. She chewed, eyes closed, and made a low hum of contentment deep in her throat, like she'd just remembered something kind from a past life.

"You want a bottle of water to go with that?" Hawthorne offered.

Twister held up a hand—to bless her, or to halt her, unclear.

"You'll need to listen soon, girl-with-the-flame-in-her-hands," she said, suddenly solemn again. "Blood's gonna fall quiet, and the sky's teeth will open. When they do, you pick your kitchen, and you choose who sits at the fire. Remember that."

Hawthorne blinked. "Is... is that...a metaphor, or should I be digging a root cellar?"

Twister didn't answer. She stuffed the remaining half of the sandwich into the pocket of her coat—next to what looked, unsettlingly, like a deflated condom—and gave Hawthorne a wink.

Then she gave the broomstick a jaunty twirl over one shoulder like a bindle, pivoted on her taped-up boots, and started to shuffle away, singing some unrecognizable tune that sounded vaguely like "Take Me Out to the Ball Game" if all the vowels had been stolen in a scrabble heist.

Hawthorne stood there a moment longer, watching her go. Overhead, the sky was still clouded over in its usual early-spring grumpiness, the kind of reflected light that made everything feel a few shades softer and a little more tired.

She shook her head and turned back toward the truck.

"Choose who sits at the fire," she muttered to herself. "Alright, Tori Amos Cryptid... I'll just pencil that one between checking the fryer oil and dodging Frank's toxic masculinity."

As she rounded the corner again, the faint pop of laughter floated from the quad. A student in a Pikachu hoodie was balancing a large box of seedlings like a tightrope walker. For now, at least for this one small, crispy-on-the-outside, chaos-on-the-inside moment, everything was fine.

The world was still turning, the sky hadn't sprouted teeth, and

Hawthorne's kitchen-on-wheels? If it was on fire, it was probably Frank's fault.

She cracked her knuckles, took a deep breath, and slid into the truck through the back step.

Rucha didn't even look up.

"Good timing," she said, flipping a ticket over. "Frank's sulking in the cab 'researching local ordinances.' Also known as Googling 'can you get fined for hurt feelings.'"

Hawthorne grinned and tied her apron back on. "Well, it's good to be needed. Even if the worms and frogs know something we don't."

Rucha laughed before turning back to the crowd at the order window.

By the time the lunch rush petered out and the last few sleepy students had shuffled away to class, Hawthorne's shirt was dotted with grease and aioli, her arms were aching, and her brain buzzed like a fridge light half-burning out.

Frank had disappeared somewhere along the way, ostensibly to "handle the supply chain crisis," but Hawthorne suspected he was nearby, sulking in his car with the AC blasting and playing an aggressive round of Candy Crush in his sad little realm of managerial delusion. Rucha wiped down the prep station with the kind of slow, meditative intensity only someone repressing a scream could muster while Hawthorne finished packing up the cooking station and securing supplies.

"You're driving the truck, right?" Hawthorne asked, hanging up her apron.

"Yeah yeah yeah. I'm pretty sure Frank is gonna tail me the whole way." She sighed heavily. "You heading home?" she asked as Hawthorne shrugged on a denim jacket that still smelled lightly of barbecue and cinnamon.

"Yeah. I've reached my quota for unsolicited life advice and sandwich-related prophecies, and I need a nap."

Rucha snorted. "Try not to get caught in the kale uprising on your way."

"I've trained for it. I was in the gifted program."

She gave Rucha a salute, half-meant, and stepped down onto the sidewalk with a satisfying thump of her boots. A cool breeze whispered down from the hills skirting Fairhope, tugging playfully at the flyaways escaping her loose ponytail.

The walk home took fifteen minutes, twenty if she didn't feel like dodging the tours given by the Student Ambassadors who liked to march around campus with backwards-worn baseball caps and unnerving amounts of enthusiasm. Today, she opted for the long way, cutting through a block of houses with deep porches and creaky porch swings that rocked even when empty, as though memory sat down and never left.

Her and her mother's house sat at the edge of Magnolia Place, once a shiny ribbon of modest middle-class comfort in Fairhope's older east side. That shine had dulled over time. The tornado event of '07 hadn't helped, nor had three consecutive mayors who prioritized highways over housing. Now, the sidewalks were cracked, the stucco a bit mold-licked, and there was always a faint scent of someone grilling something too early or too late in the day.

Their little 1940s concrete block bungalow had planters along the sidewalk, filled with petunias and creeping thyme. Marla's doing. There were also three mismatched wind chimes on the porch, one made of chipped china teacups and another that had originally been part of a capiz chandelier from the short-lived Filipino fusion place that used to be downtown. Hawthorne may or may not have made off with it the night the restaurant closed down (without notice and without paying the staff what they were owed). She would never tell. It clicked soothingly as she opened the screen door, which let out a familiar wheeze before banging shut behind her.

Inside, the place smelled like eucalyptus, rose water, and the telltale tang of Tiger Balm—Marla's standard scent cocktail. The front room held more plants than furniture: ivy trailed down from every window, spider plants formed a kind of leafy perimeter around the sagging purple thrift-store couch, and a proud pothos wove its way across the top of the bookcase like it was auditioning for a nature documentary.

"Baby-bug?" Marla's voice floated out from the hallway, buttery and sweet with just a hint of creaky charm.

“In the flesh,” Hawthorne called back, slipping off her boots and wiggling her aching toes with audible relief.

Marla appeared from the hallway draped in one of her favorite muumuus, the indigo one with little constellations embroidered along the hem, and a gauzy shawl that trailed behind her like smoke. Her gray curls were arranged in a soft, barely-there chignon, and she held a mug of ginger tea with both palms like it was an offering to the gods of joint relief.

“You look tired,” she said, and then gave a knowing little smile. “But your aura’s a bit more lemon-sunshine today. Did Frank spontaneously combust?”

“Alas, no.” Hawthorne trudged toward the old recliner by the window and collapsed into it. “But I did get yelled at, saved a sandwich from a tragic end, and exchanged cryptic warnings with Fairhope’s most elusive prophet.”

Marla’s brow lifted in amusement. “Twister?”

“Mmm-hmm. She said something about kitchen bones and choosing who sits at the fire. Also, something about teeth in the sky.” Hawthorne sighed, closing her eyes for a second. “Sometimes I wish I could live in her world. It doesn’t have time cards or health violations or Frank.”

“Well, in her world, the frogs are spies and the moon might explode. So maybe a healthy enough dose of here and now is still good for your chakras,” Marla said gently, easing into the other chair with a soft grunt that spoke of stiffness and routine. Her arthritis had gotten worse over winter, and though she’d never say it directly, Hawthorne could see the shift in the slope of her shoulders, the way she moved with deliberate slowness. Her mother had never bounced back after the death of her husband of thirty years, and it made Hawthorne feel like she was sometimes mourning the loss of two people instead of one. Yet, her mother was still with her and still took care of Hawthorne as best she could.

There was silence for a moment, filled only by the hum of the old house and the rhythm of leaves shifting in the breeze outside. Marla reached over to the side table between them and produced a small, battered tin. “I made lemon balm cookies. With chamomile, not that sleepy time commercial nonsense, the good stuff from the back porch planter. You want one?"

Hawthorne cracked one eye open and gave a faint, lopsided grin. "Only if you didn't bake them while communing with Mercury in retrograde again, or whatever."

Marla rolled her eyes but handed her a cookie anyway. "I see your stomach doesn't mind my astrology when it's wrapped in butter and sugar."

They sat in companionable stillness as the late afternoon light slipped in through the window, dappled by the leafy tendrils of the ivy. Hawthorne nibbled her cookie slowly, savoring the taste of soft, herbal sweetness with a warm vanilla note underneath. Her limbs still ached from the morning rush, and her brain still thrummed with low-grade exhaustion, but somehow the stillness made all of it feel a little less heavy. Like maybe today didn't have to mean anything bigger than this.

"What's really bothering you, baby-bug?" Her mother patted her arm softly.

"I feel like a loser whenever we work on campus," she murmured, not quite intending to say it aloud. "I see all those students going to classes and making something out of their lives while I serve up another jackfruit melt." She felt bad as soon as she said it, knowing what her mother would say next.

"I'm sorry I had to ask you to help with your father when he was sick. You should have stayed in college," she said mournfully.

"No, I'm glad I could help. And honestly, I could restart classes if I really wanted, but now I'm not sure I want to. I don't actually know what I want to do, is the problem, Mama."

Her mother hummed, leaving space for Hawthorne to keep talking.

"Sometimes I talk with Rucha about opening our own restaurant. She's going for that accounting degree, and she has all those years of helping her father and older sisters run the motel. But I just cook. I love it, but...I feel like everyone else is building something and I'm just... patching holes with duct tape and dreams."

Marla smiled, soft and sure. "Duct tape has held this country together for a hundred years, honey. Dreams are just the reinforcement."

And in that slanted golden hush of a beautiful spring evening, it was almost enough.

CHAPTER 2
Something's Not Right

The morning was pale and hazy, the kind of day that made Hawthorne feel like she was moving through a watercolor painting, colors bleeding into one another, soft but lacking definition. The air was thick with the scent of jasmine swaying on a light breeze, and she found herself leaning against the side of The Gourmet Grinder, staring into space as she brought the bag of fresh basil up to her nose to take a refreshing sniff.

"Earth to Hawthorne!" Rucha called, her cheerful voice piercing through the morning fog that seemed to have settled in right on top of Hawthorne's spirits. She popped out from the back door of the truck, clutching a huge mug of coffee as if it were a trophy. "You're not zoning out on me again, are you?"

Hawthorne blinked, shaking off her moment of introspection. "Sorry, I was just—"

"Contemplating your life choices?" Rucha finished for her, her voice somehow both teasing and supportive. "That's a dangerous rabbit hole, friend. We need to save that for when we crack open the wine tonight."

"Yeah, well, it's easy to feel out of place when you're not sure where you're supposed to be," Hawthorne muttered, not entirely keeping the weariness from her tone.

Rucha slid a familiar, reassuring arm around Hawthorne's shoulders, pulling her close for a moment. "You get like this every time we roll up on Hayden's campus, but honestly? You're doing fine! You keep this whole operation afloat, even with Frank being a pain in the ass."

Hawthorne snorted a laugh at that. She knew that she was the reason The Gourmet Grinder was as successful as it was, but it wasn't enough to drown out the nagging feeling of inadequacy that even her mother's cookies could not dispel. Five years ago, she had been so certain she would graduate with a major in something *important*, and become someone her dad was proud of, but instead she was getting ready to work another shift in a food truck after huffing on fresh basil.

"I should be working on my future instead of trying to keep Frank from self-destructing every ten minutes," Hawthorne continued as she followed Rucha into the truck then busied herself arranging storage bins full of freshly sliced vegetables.

"Oh, please," Rucha scoffed, adjusting her neon green bandanna with an exaggerated flair. "You've turned saving Frank into an extreme sport. Is there a medal for that? If so, I'm definitely getting some kind of award for surviving his rants about proper food labeling."

Hawthorne half-laughed, half-sighed, appreciating Rucha's attempt to pull her out of her funk. She knew the older woman was just trying to keep spirits high, but the weight of her own unrealized aspirations pressed heavier today than usual.

"You're right. I mean, he's a handful, but... sometimes I think about how I was just a kid when all this changed. When Dad got sick."

Rucha leaned against the prep counter, her expression softening as she crossed her arms over her denim jacket. "It was a lot for anyone to handle. You took care of him. You did what you needed to do. Even my mother could not fault your filial piety! But I promise you, it's not like there's a deadline to get your life back on track. Some of us take a little longer to get where we're going. I've been in and out of college three times already. Heck, I'm pretty sure I've switched majors more times than I've changed my shampoo."

"Yeah, but you have that fire in you. You're taking charge. You've finally picked a track and have a plan! I just keep grilling sandwiches."

"Hey." Rucha's tone turned serious. "Look at me." When

Hawthorne met her gaze, Rucha continued, "You're strong, Hawthorne. You rolled with the punches when it mattered most. It doesn't matter if you're working food trucks or doing something else. What matters is that you're making a difference, even if it feels small."

"Even 'small' seems overwhelming right now." Hawthorne picked at the corner of a tray as a nervous habit. The sunlight glinted off her hands, still stained with remnants of yesterday's work with pickled beets.

Apparently sensing the shift in her energy, Rucha chuckled knowingly. "I told you we're gonna open our own bistro, didn't I? But first" —she punctuated her words by motioning to the stacks of bok choy ready for wash—"time to prep!"

Hawthorne took a deep breath, letting Rucha's reassuring words settle like a cool breeze. "Yeah, you're right. Let's just get through today, and we'll figure it out later."

The clock ticked closer to eleven, and Rucha began wheeling out The Gourmet Grinder sign, a brightly painted piece of chalkboard that read: "Feeding the Future—One Wrap at a Time!" She worked with quick, short bursts of energy as she set the scene for the impending lunch crowd.

"Looking good!" Hawthorne called as she sprinkled water on the grill to test the heat. The splattering sound accompanied Rucha's effervescent energy, the kind that could only come from someone primed for a busy day ahead. Everything about this routine felt so normal that for a moment, it pushed back the shadows of frustration lurking in the corners of Hawthorne's mind. She was there to cook, and that was something she *knew* she was good at.

Just as the first few tentative students began to snake their way toward the window, the unmistakable sound of a revving engine cut through the morning calm. Before long, Frank's massive, too-clean pickup truck pulled into view, and her temporary tranquility evaporated.

Frank stormed out of the truck, an indignant expression plastered across his face like it was part of an official uniform.

"What are you standing around for?" he barked as he approached, chest puffed up. "You two are supposed to have the truck ready to go! We're not running a charity here. This is a business!"

Hawthorne exchanged an exasperated glance with Rucha. "We're ready, Frank. Just preparing for lunch, as usual." She tried to keep her tone professional even as she fought the urge to roll her eyes.

"Yeah, well, 'as usual' isn't good enough right now!" His voice rose, grating against her ears. "You need to act like you're serious about this job. We have a reputation to uphold! I won't tolerate laziness or distraction today, understood? Thursday is always our busiest day. We need to be focused!"

"Understood," Rucha said with mock politeness, planting her hands on her hips.

Frank narrowed his eyes, clearly unfazed by her sarcasm. "This isn't a game, Rucha. We need to maximize profit and efficiency. Let's get it together." With that, he disappeared into the cab again, mumbling something about "proper business practices."

As soon as he was out of earshot, Hawthorne let out a long-suffering sigh. "I swear, he treats us like we're a couple of toddlers playing dress-up instead of running the food truck his daddy bought for him."

"Maybe we should just accept it and start wearing tutu skirts next shift. Then he'll really think we're running a circus." Rucha rolled her eyes dramatically as she flicked a stray bundle of herbs out of the way. "Or tell him we're resigning and joining Twister's spiritual guide adventure tour."

Hawthorne chuckled, the weight in her chest lightening, if only for a moment. "Now that sounds like a plan."

Rucha leaned over the counter, a conspiratorial smirk sliding onto her face. "We could serve kale smoothies served with a side of prophetic doom."

Hawthorne laughed, and as the two of them exchanged more sarcastic banter, the first wave of customers converged on the truck, a mix of students with lunch breaks and academic staff hoping to grab a quick bite.

Just as some enthusiasm tinged the air, a woman approached the window, her features pinched and uninviting. She may have had a friendly tone, but her words dripped with the kind of expectation that set Hawthorne on edge. "What's taking so long? I thought food trucks were supposed to be quick! I have a class in ten minutes."

"Sorry for the delay, ma'am." Rucha smiled politely, her voice bright and rehearsed. "What can I get for you today?"

"I've heard mixed reviews about this place." The woman stared down her nose as if trying to peer into the very essence of Hawthorne's soul. "I've seen better service at a funeral home."

A sharp laugh bubbled up in Hawthorne's throat, and she quickly swallowed it down. "We have barbecue tofu wraps, jackfruit melts, and some delicious herb salads!" she offered, her tone light-hearted yet strained.

The woman's lip curled, assessing the menu as if it were the latest release from a low-brow chef. "Tofu? Ugh. I'll just have the jackfruit melt, extra crispy. And make it fast."

"Coming right up," Hawthorne chirped, fighting to keep the annoyance from seeping into her voice. As she turned to prepare the order, she caught Rucha's eye, a burst of shared exasperation lighting up the space between them.

"Extra crispy?" Rucha echoed, barely keeping her composure. "I'll see what I can do but just be warned—too crispy is basically charred around here."

The woman crossed her arms impatiently, and Hawthorne could practically see the gears in her brain grinding to a halt, trying to comprehend the humor. The atmosphere of camaraderie felt as tenuous as a piece of buttered toast on the edge of a table. As always, she had to remind herself to take the high road, just as her father taught her, but it was something she grew increasingly weary of, particularly when faced with the likes of belligerent customers.

Sliding the jackfruit onto the grill, she forced a smile, hoping it could somehow bridge the gulf of annoyance between them. "We promise it'll be delicious, ma'am. Just a moment!"

The first sweet notes of the jackfruit started to waft through the truck, filling the air with a blend of spices that reminded Hawthorne of late summer picnics and her mother's popular backyard barbecues. Maybe a hint of warmth would smooth some of the tension hovering around them.

"Make sure you add enough slaw," the woman barked again, her demeanor suggesting she was the queen of a particularly demanding territory.

"Right away, your majesty," Hawthorne muttered under her breath, narrowly suppressing an eye roll.

Rucha leaned back to catch a view of the cooktop, watching the jackfruit. "Like I said, total circus," she whispered, giving Hawthorne an absurdly exaggerated wink.

Finally, with the order plated, she handed it out, curtailing her more sarcastic impulses. "Here you go! Enjoy!"

As the woman took her melt, her eyes narrowed into a skeptical squint. "I expect it to be good. Otherwise, I'm leaving a scathing review online."

"Fantastic," Rucha replied, voice dripping with faux cheer. "That's how we measure success around here. One tearful online review at a time."

The woman glared at them and tossed her hair back dramatically before marching away, jackfruit melt held high like a trophy.

As she retreated, Rucha burst out laughing, a fresh wave of energy filling the air again. "You know what this means? We've officially had our first rude and passive-aggressive customer of the day! We can check it off the list."

The lunch rush transformed The Gourmet Grinder into a whirlwind of noise and activity. Orders flew with the speed of verbal daggers, tossed out on snippets of laughter and the occasional friendly banter between Rucha and the customers. The air thickened with the scent of sizzling vegetables and tangy aioli, blending seamlessly.

Hawthorne danced between the griddle and the service window, her movements fluid even as her exhaustion clawed at her. "Order for Zach! Extra pickles!" she called out while deftly flipping the tofu onto the hot surface, listening for its satisfying sizzle when she plopped it on the griddle. Just behind her, Rucha was an orchestra conductor of chaos, relaying orders, clearing out trash, and laughing about the absurdity of Frank's latest meltdown to a gaggle of eager students waiting for their food.

Hawthorne caught the eyes of a guy waiting at the counter, shirt a little more fitted than his demeanor suggested, and it took a moment before she recognized him as one of the philosophy majors from her father's old university connections. She assumed he was faculty now. He looked both bemused and slightly terrified, munching on a crispy tofu wrap as if savoring the complexity of the flavors. She couldn't help but feel a surge of pride in their food when he gave her a thumbs-up.

As lunchtime progressed, she and Rucha shifted like a well-oiled machine, moving in tight sync honed through countless busy shifts.

"Hey, I'm out of slaw! Can you grab a few more batches from the back fridge?" Rucha shouted, never pausing in her charming chatter, slipping small digs into the conversation with each customer while she mixed up custom orders like a magician pulling rabbits from hats.

"Coming right up!" Hawthorne called back, ducking down into the cramped quarters of the food truck fridge. She momentarily lost herself in counting the greens, regretting their current lettuce situation—want to make every dish count, after all.

Just outside, a lively line formed, students engaged in distracted conversation, noses buried in their phones. Hawthorne handed off two grinders and caught snippets of laughter and playful debates about which classes had semi-popular professors. She leaned into the rhythm of the rush, her laughter spilling forth as she exchanged playful retorts with her customers.

The sun climbed higher, bathing the truck in a pool of warmth, and it felt as if the world outside their window expanded with boundless energy. This was when Hawthorne felt most alive, lost in a whirlwind of flavors, connections, and laughter. There was something magical in the air, almost electric, filling her lungs with optimism despite the tumult around her.

As things began to settle a bit more, the cadence of her kitchen dance slowed as the lunch hour began to wind down. As the last lingering orders began to fade into the ether, she spotted Leo Foxx approaching alongside Carlos, one of his graduate students. With Leo's steady demeanor, a precise and deliberate stride, and Carlos's tall frame bound by a shy but contagious smile, they were a collision of comfort and curiosity. They were both dressed in what Hawthorne's mother called the "Agri Uniform," which was straight legged jeans and a thrifted long-sleeve button up shirt over a light-colored tee shirt, topped off with a battered baseball hat bearing farm equipment logo. The result was something resembling a cross between Americana farmer chic and lazy undergrad.

"Look who it is!" Rucha squealed, her voice tinged with playful excitement as she leaned dramatically out from the service window like a performer making a grand entrance. "If it isn't our favorite agriculture expert and his adorable lackey!"

Leo chuckled and glanced over at Hawthorne. When their eyes met, a jovial light flickered in his, making Hawthorne duck back into the truck like a teenager with a crush. It was embarrassing but she could not help feeling wrong-footed around the handsome faculty member.

"I wouldn't go that far, Rucha. Just here for sustenance," he grinned, tapping his chin, an almost scholarly deliberation in his gaze.

"Right, sustenance in the form of flavor-bursting grinders, but we all know you're really here for the *fixings*," Rucha replied with a smirk. "How's your new garden project shaping up, Carlos? You sure you haven't been growing charming dorkiness along with those plants?" She gave Carlos a long once-over, making the timid man blush straight through his dark complexion.

Hawthorne's heart fluttered as Rucha effortlessly flirted with Carlos, teasingly dragging him along into their banter. It was a deft move that made her skin tingle with the slightest hint of jealousy. Hawthorne quickly busied herself at the griddle, flipping a crispy hash patty while trying to project both competence and casual confidence, even as a nervous warmth crept up her neck when Leo's gaze flicked back to her.

"Borderline disaster, honestly," Leo replied, his tone self-deprecating as he adjusted his hat. "I think the cucumbers might be staging a takeover. So, you'll save me a sandwich for my vegetables' rebellion?"

"I don't know, I'm always down for a revolution of the vegetable labor class," Rucha declared, placing her hands on her hips dramatically. "But I'm sure Hawthorne will whip you up something blessed straight from the harvest."

"More like straight from the griddle," Hawthorne said with a chuckle as she scraped up a batch of crispy hash and prepared to plate it up. Feeling momentarily bold, she decided to lean into the playful energy. "You've probably just earned a fruit fly army for your troubles if you don't watch your garden closely. Not all heroes wear lab coats, you know."

Leo raised an eyebrow, his lips quirking at the corners with a hint of mischief. "Well, someone needs to keep an eye on the ecosystem around here. If things get too chaotic, we'll send in the expert—Twister, perhaps? An environmental intervention might be in order."

"Let's not encourage her," Rucha chimed in. "The last thing we need is her declaring a holy war against inadequate composting efforts."

Hawthorne finished plating the grinders for the two students standing anxiously next to Leo, her heart fluttering just a bit as she noticed him watching her the way he did, like he appreciated the small things. "Two jackfruit melts, one side of crispy hash!" She turned to him as the students grabbed their paper baskets and, presumably, ran for class.

He opened his mouth to say something but was cut short by Twister, her presence crashing into their midday rhythm like a thunderclap. From the other side of the quad, she appeared with the fervor of a hurricane, limbs flailing wildly and hat askew, her wild white hair like a crown of storm clouds.

"THE HORIZON IS BURNING!" she bellowed, voice crackling with the weight of an ancient storm as she marched toward them, broomstick raised like a talisman against dark days ahead. "DANGER'S SHADOWS SWIM IN THE KITCHENS OF MEN, AND THE MEAT MYTH IS A LIE!"

Hawthorne's heart sank as she exchanged a glance with Leo and Rucha. This time, there was no trace of humor in Twister's eyes, only an unsettling fervor that sent chills down Hawthorne's spine.

"Seriously?" Rucha muttered, as Twister's words shattered the lightheartedness of the lunch rush, casting a pall over their flavors and laughter. "That's new."

As Twister continued her prophetic tirade, it felt as if the very air thickened with unease, choking back the joy they had created in their little food truck. "COUNT THE DEAD AS THEY RISE! THE EARTH WILL SHUDDER, AND YOU WILL WISH FOR THE

WARMTH OF THE SUN'S BREATH! WHO WILL FEED THE ONES WHO ARE NO LONGER WHO THEY SEEM?"

"Uh... Twister?" Hawthorne called out of the window tentatively, unsure if interrupting her would invite more chaos or the satisfaction of being heard.

But Twister didn't pause. In fact, she picked up speed, her voice soaring above the sounds of rattling frying pans and muffled laughter. "THE GARDEN WILL GROW DAMNED! TEETH IN THE RAPTURE! BRING YOUR FEAST TO THE SHADOWS OR FIND YOUR HEART INSIDE A DARK CAULDRON!"

The absurdity of her words twisted like sharp blades at the edges of their minds, and Hawthorne felt a deep pit ache in her stomach as the usual part of her brain that found humor in Twister's premonitions went ominously still. The other students who lined up behind Leo and Carlos had turned, faces drawn tight in confusion or fear as they processed what had just interrupted their lunch hour.

"Uh, right. So..." Leo rubbed the back of his neck awkwardly, trying to navigate the sudden shift in atmosphere as he stepped forward to talk to the deranged woman. "Twister, any chance you can...um, take your show on the road? They're trying to serve food here."

Unfazed by the light distraction, Twister continued to ramp up her performance, her voice echoing ominously. "FALL ON YOUR KNEES AND SOW THE SEEDS OF CAUTION, FOR THIS IS ONLY THE BEGINNING!"

With a dramatic flourish, she waved her broomstick and then, as quickly as she had arrived, abruptly pivoted on her heel and shuffled away, leaving a mixture of confusion and amusement in her wake. The once-lively atmosphere around The Gourmet Grinder faded, and for a moment, no one dared speak, the ripples of Twister's voice hanging thickly in the air.

"Okay, then," Carlos said, breaking the silence with a tentative chuckle. "If she's right, though, should we put extra slaw on the apocalypse specials?"

"Extra slaw for extra drama," Rucha quipped, finally breaking free of the weight that had settled between them and dispelling the shadow of Twister's stranger-than-usual rant.

"That would definitely sell better than the usual fare, I bet," Leo added, shaking off the heaviness with a chuckle, the tension lifting just enough for the rhythm of both their banter and the truck's busy service to pick back up.

As the customers resumed ordering, Hawthorne gave her head a brisk shake and dove back into work. But Leo's presence remained like an anchor for her spirit, and for the first time that morning, she felt a smile creeping back onto her lips.

"Looks like we survived the first half of the day," she said, plating up Carlos's grinder (with extra slaw on the side). "What could go wrong?"

"Never say that!" Rucha shrieked, causing Carlos to cringe backward from the pickup window. Hawthorne picked up the paper basket and held it out for him encouragingly.

As he leaned forward to accept his lunch, his eyes drifted toward the horizon and then narrowed. "Okay," he said slowly, craning his neck toward the open plaza. "That's not normal."

"What?" Hawthorne glanced up, but didn't see anything at first, just the usual sunbaked bricks of the quad, half-empty coffee cups on study tables, and students lazily lounging under sunshades. But Carlos pointed again, this time with urgency.

"Look, west side. Above the buildings."

Hawthorne, Leo, and Rucha followed his finger. A bank of clouds was incoming fast. Too fast. One moment, it was sunshine and the next, an unnatural mass of storm was rolling in like a living thing. The deep greens and bruise-like purples smeared the sky, and lightning flashed within it, branching in jagged, corkscrewed patterns like something alive and searching.

Rucha squinted at the sky. "Did we miss a forecast or something? That storm looks... pissed off."

Carlos squinted. "That's tornado weather." His voice was tight. "I've seen that look before, back home in Kansas. Those cloud spirals don't mess around. We need to get people under shelter."

Leo turned slowly toward the churning skyline. "Storm systems don't usually move that fast. This is—"

"Wrong. It's wrong," Carlos finished, suddenly scanning the plaza with renewed urgency.

Around them, others were taking notice. Students paused mid-conversation, eyes lifting skyward as wind hissed through the oak trees. Umbrellas snapped inside out, and the first ominous rumble cracked through the air, deep, low, and not at all like thunder usually sounded.

"What the hell is that?" Rucha asked, her voice barely audible as she leaned out farther over the window's counter.

The mood in the plaza shifted as laughter died down, giving way to a rising murmur of unease. Someone shouted, "Check the weather app!" and within moments, a wave of glowing phone screens popped into view.

"No alerts?" someone called. "That can't be right. There's definitely lightning."

"Guys," Hawthorne said slowly, stepping away from the window toward the prep station. "I don't like this."

At the front of the truck, Frank stood up from the driver's seat and walked into the prep area, looking irritated rather than alarmed. "What are we doing? There's still a quarter of the lunch crowd out there! Don't go shutting things down just because the sky threw on a Halloween costume!"

Hawthorne wanted to snap something about how ominous green-purple skies shouldn't be dismissed like a wilted lettuce, but the heavy pressure in the air held her tongue. Something in her gut was humming now, low and taut, like the pluck of a string just before it snaps.

She turned back to the others, eyes scanning the plaza. Across the open square, students were rising from benches and study spots with uncertain expressions. Some walked backward slowly, filming the sky on their phones. Others gathered in small groups, murmuring over weather apps that still displayed nothing more than a bright cartoon sun and a gentle breeze icon.

Carlos stepped closer, his tone shifting from mild concern to urgency. "We've got maybe two minutes, tops, before that hits." He gestured toward the leading edge of the cloud. "We should be getting underground, now."

Rucha stared at him, wide-eyed. Her playfulness was gone. "Underground? There is no underground! We're in a truck, on a brick plaza, surrounded by classroom and Wi-Fi. What, you want us to burrow into the recycling bins?"

Lightning cracked again—louder this time—and the sound it made didn't just echo. It vibrated. Deep in her chest, Hawthorne felt it rattle between her ribs like something searching, probing.

Frank barked from the front. "You pack up this truck before we're done, and I'll dock both your hours."

"You're about to lose more than hours if you keep your head in the sand," Hawthorne snapped back.

Leo stepped closer to the window, his voice low and calm. "Frank," he said, hands raised slightly in peace. "Look around. This storm is moving fast. There's lightning with no thunder, and people are starting to panic. Don't you think we should at least get to safety?"

The sky broke open.

Not with rain, but with *sound*. A wave of noise howled through the plaza, sharp and mechanical, something between a siren and a scream. Phones dropped. Bags hit the ground. Every bird in every tree took flight at once, their wings fluttering in chaotic, terrified harmony.

Hawthorne's hand shot out instinctively, grabbing Rucha's arm as the wind hit and rocked the truck. Rucha didn't need another word. The instant Hawthorne yanked her arm, she followed, bolting down from the service window platform. Hawthorne threw open the back door and yelled out.

"Better than nothing! Get in!"

Leo and Carlos scrambled into the truck while Frank bitched about it, Leo slamming the swinging side door shut just as the storm's ghostly moan swept over the plaza with what felt like a tidal wave of pressure.

The wind came alive. Not like weather but more like a living presence. Tables were upturned in seconds, papers and wrappers and notebooks whirling into the air like frantic birds. Trees bent, not swayed. They cracked. One of the nearby tents from the geography club's information booth was lifted and hurled across the bricks in a tumbling arc before colliding with the side of a statue and crumpling like tissue.

Inside the truck, the metal vibrated, the walls pulsing with each beat of whatever sound the storm was emitting. It was not just loud, it was wrong. The frequencies hit Hawthorne like needles behind the eyes, drilling into her skull and settling between her thoughts.

Rucha gasped.

Hawthorne turned from looking out the front window to see Frank by the rear storage fridge. She realized that he hadn't moved since they all retreated inside the truck, not when the screaming started outside, not when the wind turned feral and glass shattered across campus. He had stayed rooted where he stood, mouth open, eyes distant like a tape loop frozen at the edge of static.

He wasn't right.

"Frank?" Hawthorne's voice cracked under the strain of the noise outside, causing Leo to look at her then turn to focus on Frank in the back. But it was the silence that made her breath catch in her throat.

He twitched.

One sharp jerk of the shoulder, like a puppet's string had been pulled too hard.

His neck stretched unnaturally to the side, accompanied by a sickening series of wet pops. The skin along his jaw began to turn colors. Not pale but dark gray. Blotchy. Like bruises blossoming underwater.

"Dios mío," Carlos whispered, backing up and pulling Rucha with him.

Frank twitched again, this time his fingers flexing as if from electric shocks. Then both his hands began trembling in short, violent bursts. His eyes fluttered, rolled, then fixed on nothing.

Frank's body snapped into motion like a spring uncoiling—violent, unexplained, and full of raw malice. One moment he was sagging, twitching in place, and the next he was lurching across the prep floor with a low, guttural groan that didn't sound human. It didn't even sound animal.

It sounded hungry.

"Frank! No!" Rucha shouted, backing away instinctively, hands raised, but she was too slow. Carlos shoved her to the side and Frank slammed into him, catching him by the shoulder with a clawing grip. His fingers didn't curl like a normal fist, they jabbed, stiff and sharp like hooked twigs tearing through Carlos's overshirt. Carlos let out a strangled cry as blood bloomed crimson against the dark fabric of his tee shirt. He stumbled, tripping on the rubber mat, face twisted in pain and panic.

"Get off him!" Hawthorne shouted, the biggest prep knife already in hand from the prep counter. Without thinking, without pausing to consider the weight of what she was about to do, she lunged and slashed, cleaving across Frank's arm with a kitchen knife honed to perfection. It sunk in with a sickening resistance before meeting slick, unnatural ease. Like cutting into rotten fruit.

Frank screamed, or maybe it was just air escaping his lungs, a sound of pain and outrage.

"Hawthorne, stop! He's not human anymore!" Rucha cried, shoving herself between them, broom in hand. She jammed the brush-end of it into his chest like she was making a medieval stand against a siege.

Frank staggered, briefly halting, but not for long. With a horrifying shudder, he leaned forward, snapping his teeth inches from Rucha's face, his jaw clacking closed like a steel trap. His skin was tinged green-gray now, slimy with sweat, and black lines spread across his arms like roots tearing through parchment.

"Leo!" Hawthorne shouted, frantic, glancing at the side door they'd come in through.

"I'm going!" Leo bolted, yanking the front door open with both hands and flinging himself back outside into the shrieking wind of the storm, disappearing from Hawthorne's view.

Inside, Frank howled and tried lunging again. Rucha shouted something unintelligible and jabbed the broom harder, teeth bared as she pushed with every ounce of her strength. "Keep him back!" Hawthorne reached around Rucha's waist and also grabbed the handle, both of them driving the broomstick into his stomach to keep pushing him back.

Frank's movements grew even *more* jerky as he fought, but his arms beat at the broom like a child trying to swat a fly. His mouth gaped open, drooling, teeth slick with spit and something darker. The hiss that came from his throat was wet and desperate, and it turned Hawthorne's stomach more than the attack itself.

The back of the truck rattled twice and then with a shrieking clatter, the rolling door yanked upward.

"Now!" Leo shouted, his voice cutting through the chaos.

Hawthorne and Rucha shoved as one, using the long broom handle like a makeshift battering ram. Frank staggered, heels slipping on leftover bits of slaw now slick with Carlos's blood.

"One more!" Rucha gasped, and they gave a final, desperate heave.

Frank toppled backward, howling as he hit the brick pavers and bounced a little. His arms flailed behind him like a marionette whose strings had been cut.

Hawthorne's chest heaved, burnt air searing her lungs.

"Leo!" she screamed.

Leo was already leaping backward, grabbing the roller handle with one hand and yanking it down with all his weight. The grooved door slammed with a brutal metallic thud, locking just as Frank—with impossible speed—lunged back upright against the outside of the door, slamming it with a deafening crack.

Rucha collapsed backward onto her hands, breath ragged. "Please tell me that worked."

Leo stumbled away from the door, chest heaving. "It did. He's out."

Thump.

The door shuddered.

Thump.

Carlos groaned behind them, clutching his wounded arm. "What the hell was that? What the hell is he?"

"We're gonna deal with that! We're all gonna be okay," Hawthorne said, dodging the churning whine of her thoughts. She looked at her knife on the floor, slick with gore.

Outside, the storm roared louder.

CHAPTER 3
Left Behind

Hawthorne couldn't get the blood off her hands.

She had wiped them as thoroughly as she could. First on a paper towel, then on her apron, then using regular disinfectant cleaning wipes when the towel wouldn't do. Still, her palms felt warm and sticky, like the knife had left something there beyond the smear of Frank's blood, as if it had filled the lines of her skin with something that didn't wash out.

The storm outside beat against the metal shell of the truck like it was trying to claw its way in. The wind keened, high and shrill, a wounded sound that pierced right through the thin, shallow breaths she was trying to take in.

No one spoke—not Rucha, not Leo, not even Carlos, who crouched in the corner with a wad of sterile napkins clutched to his bleeding arm. It smelled like iron and onion inside the truck. The grill, now off, took too long to cool. Hawthorne could still hear the last sputtering trails of heat from the grill plate, like the final fizz of something dying.

Then came a shriek from outside.

Hawthorne's head snapped toward Leo instinctively, but he was already moving, inching into the cab where the front windshield sat fogged and flickering with dull stormlight. Rucha hesitated, then joined him, and Hawthorne's feet followed without her asking them.

They crowded into the cab, Hawthorne taking the driver's seat which was the only chair, the others crouched like kids caught in a thunderstorm under their mom's coffee table. Rucha took a handful of papertowels and wiped down the window to clear the fog. They peered out.

The view hit her like a glass of ice water to the face.

The quad was gone?

No, it was still there, brick-lined and tree-guarded and ringed with old stone benches. But it had changed, as if it had been twisted and rung out.

Crumpled white stone from a broken statue lay in chunks across the far path, as if a boulder had landed there and exploded. Tables were overturned and a couple of table umbrellas had been ripped from their moorings and bent around railings like tinfoil. Stains were on the bricks, dark blooms that hadn't been there ten minutes ago.

Bodies.

At first, Hawthorne saw them only as weird shapes until it hit her that they were *people.* Some hunched, some limp, some crawling in ways that made her stomach twist.

"Is that—is that a fucking *zombie*?" Rucha whispered.

"Y-yeah," Leo said, voice clipped, low. "Yeah, it is."

A few people were still standing, staggered like marionettes with their strings tangled with jerky, clumsy movements that twisted too harshly at the joints. One near the edge of the plaza was shirtless, his chest a mess of what looked like bruises or burns, limbs flailing as he swung aimlessly at a sapling like he couldn't remember what it was. Another bumped into a trash can and kept going, dragging the overturned bin behind him like it wasn't there.

Some of the crumpled shapes on the ground twitched, then crawled to their feet, despite missing limbs or, in one case, entrails.

And then there were the sounds.

The groaning noise was wet and rattled. Feet scraped across brick in rhythms just off from human gait. Farther out there was a chorus of them, close and overlapping, the sound of something spiraling out of control and into a shape that was nearly human, but wrong in every way that mattered.

"Oh my god," Hawthorne whispered, breath fogging the glass.

It didn't look like a horror movie. It was *real.*

Too real.

Leo was rigid beside her, one hand braced on the dash. Hawthorne barely registered it, but he had started counting under his breath. She caught the edges of numbers. "Six... seven... no. Eight. And that one's —" His mouth pressed into a tight line. "Okay. Nine."

Rucha leaned forward too far, balancing herself on the wheel, and winced at the sharp squeak it gave beneath her. "Where is everyone else?" she asked quietly. "There were like... dozens of people out here before. Where'd they all go?"

There weren't bodies thick enough to account for a crowd dispersing. No piles of limbs. No bloodbath. Just emptiness around the chaos, like the survivors had simply dropped out of the frame.

It made everything worse.

Carlos groaned from the back, and Hawthorne twisted around. He'd slumped even lower against the cabinets, face pale and half-slick with sweat. The napkins were soaked red now, and his eyes were unfocused like he was peering through mist.

"We need to do something for him," she said. "We can't just sit in here while..."

While what?

Frank lost his mind and tried to eat someone?

While the wind screamed itself inside out?

While Fairhope turned into a nightmare carnival, brick by brick?

Leo pulled back from the windshield and rubbed a hand down his jaw, the stubble making a faint rasping sound. "We stay here for now. We lock it down. We're not equipped to book it through that mess."

Hawthorne nodded but then tensed up. "Mama!" She shrieked and pulled out her phone, hands shaking all over again, the carnage outside forgotten. Her hands trembled so hard she nearly dropped the phone.

Hawthorne jabbed at the screen with one thumb, cursing when it misread the touch. She mashed the speed dial for Marla, the only contact under "Favorites," and her fingers hovered like prayer. One ring. Two.

"Come on, come on, come on," she whispered, rocking forward like sheer willpower might reach across the city faster than cell towers could.

Then:

"Hey, baby-bug."

The voice sent a rush of breath up Hawthorne's throat. She nearly sobbed with relief. "Mama," she gasped. "Are you okay? Are you safe?"

There was a beat of hesitation, then a warm chuckle, tight but not panicked. "Yes, yes. I'm tucked up in the bathroom. I've got the good towels under the door crack, a gallon of water, and my pillbox organized by moon phases, just in case. The most loyal plants are in here with me too. I figured if I'm going, I'm not going without Myrtle and the boys."

Hawthorne's eyes stung. "Okay. Okay."

"Is it bad out there?" Marla asked gently.

"We don't know what it is, but it's bad," Hawthorne replied in a tight whisper. "Frank went—he went weird. And there's people outside, but they look wrong."

Marla didn't ask for clarification, which was the worst part, she just breathed deep, like she'd already suspected something. "Then don't you dare do anything reckless. You stay where it's safe, you hear me?"

"I'm coming to you."

"Baby-bug—"

"I mean it! Just hold tight, don't leave the room, and don't answer the door for anybody." Her voice cracked. "Please."

Marla exhaled through her nose, the sound tinny through the cheap speaker. "Alright. I'll wait. But you take your time. To hell with heroics! I didn't raise a martyr; I raised a clever girl."

Hawthorne nodded, even though she knew her mother couldn't see it. "I love you."

"I love you more. Now save that courage for the road."

The call disconnected. Hawthorne sat frozen for a breath before turning back toward the others, who watched her with varying expressions of uncertainty and dread.

"She's safe. For now," she said. "She's locked herself in the bathroom with water, meds, and what I can only assume are all the houseplants she could drag in with her. She's okay, but we have to get to her."

Leo ran both hands over his face with a sigh that sounded far older than he actually was. "We don't have to do anything right this second. She's secure. That's more than most right now." He gestured out the foggy windshield. "You want to drive through that?"

Hawthorne met his eyes sharply. "If she wasn't safe, if I'd gotten on the phone and heard screaming or nothing at all, would you still want to wait?"

"That's not fair," Leo said, but his voice was low. "I'm just trying to keep all of us alive."

"And Carlos?" Rucha interjected mutely, looking back toward him. "He's bleeding a lot. Are we sure waiting helps any of us?"

Carlos stirred at the mention of his name, blinking slowly. "If it makes any difference," he rasped, "I'm cool with not dying in the taco truck."

There was a pause. Then Hawthorne let out a sound between a sob and a short laugh. "We only serve tacos on Tuesdays."

Rucha chewed her lip. "But if we go, how? Do we just... walk? There's no way the truck can move with all that crap in the streets. And we don't know what those things are, or what they'll do if they see us."

Silence again. The kind that accumulated like fog, too thick, too close, smelling faintly of cold fryer grease and fear.

Hawthorne shifted and popped open the glovebox with a jerk of her wrist. Inside was a laminated fairground map from last fall, an unopened packet of mints, a dead flashlight, and—miraculously—an old local street map, folded all to hell. She unfolded it on the dash between them, smoothing the creases with shaking fingers.

"We're ten blocks from my place," she said. "If we cut behind city hall and follow the old frontage road along Mill River, we won't hit the main streets. It'll add time, but we'll avoid downtown entirely."

Rucha glanced out the windshield again. "Avoiding downtown sounds like my love language right now."

Leo exhaled through his nose. "Assuming we can get the truck there in the first place, then what? Go somewhere else? Is anywhere safe?" He shook his head. "If it's as bad as it looks, the National Guard is being deployed as we speak. We wait for help." He pointed at the floor of the truck.

"You think sitting here is going to work out better?" Hawthorne snapped, fingers clenched around the wheel. "You want us just to hole up in this tin can and pray the universe forgets we're here?"

Leo looked like he wanted to yell, but instead he measured his breath through clenched teeth. "It's not about giving up. It's about not being stupid."

"I'm not being stupid!" she shouted, louder than she meant to. "I'm trying to get to my mother!"

His face didn't soften. "I get that. I do."

But before another word could rip free, a heavy thud slammed against the metal siding of the truck. Everyone jumped—Rucha screamed—and another impact followed, this one closer to the back door. Then pounding. Scrapes. A wheezing sound like someone trying but failing to breathe.

Carlos groaned again, louder. "Ughh. I hate to interrupt the, uh, family therapy... but I think your friend's outside."

Hawthorne turned toward the back of the truck. Through the frosted slit of a port window, a silhouette loomed, with lurching, jerking, fists slapping the side like they couldn't remember how doors worked but knew something they wanted was inside.

Frank.

His mouth no longer moved with words, just gaped and shuddered. His eyes rolled behind lids that blinked at the wrong times. He threw his shoulder into the door, then retreated too fast, catching the lip of the wheel well and collapsing sideways.

Immediately, like they'd been waiting for it, two more shadows converged on the truck walls. The insistent banging resumed.

"Okay," Leo said, all the fight leaking out into terrified resolve. "Okay, screw it. We go."

"Thought so," Hawthorne muttered, wrenching the keys from behind the visor and twisting them into the ignition. The engine coughed once, then rumbled to life.

"Rucha, tend to Carlos. Use the first aid kit. Tourniquet if you have to!" Hawthorne yelled over the engine.

"On it! It's not that bad, though, just a few claw marks--ack!" She called out as the whole truck lurched when Hawthorne threw it into reverse, nearly clipping a busted-out trash can that had rolled into their path. Hawthorne did not need a map to know where to go. She had traveled that exact route by bicycle plenty of times, so she angled the truck to a side ally and tried to keep from hitting debris.

Despite the lack of rain or wind, lightning struck around them a few times, like someone flipping on the overheads in a haunted house for one agonizing instant. Each flash lit twisted glimpses of limbs too long or faces slack with something cruel and distant.

Leo braced himself in the cab, one hand gripping the steel frame just above the windshield, the other pressed flat against the dash whenever they turned sharper than expected. He stayed silent, but his eyes flicked to her hands at the wheel, then to the road, then back, like he meant to memorize every twist of her route in case he had to take over.

In the back, Rucha talked to Carlos in steady bursts, her voice too fast and slightly too chirpy, which Hawthorne knew was her version of "stressed the fuck out." Hawthorne caught edges of their conversation —something about EMT training she dropped out of, and how her first bandaging job had been on her aunt's Pomeranian who got into a raccoon fight.

It felt absurd and perfect in that moment.

The truck growled as she turned south, tires sliding across slick asphalt. They clipped the curb behind City Hall with a jolt, and Leo muttered, "Nice one," either to her or the truck itself.

"Two inches to the left and we'd be flipped," Hawthorne muttered back, knuckles white on the wheel.

She finally made the turn onto the frontage road.

It curled like a lazy question mark along the edge of Mill River, old and narrow enough to be forgotten by most city traffic, and the kind of street no one used except delivery drivers and kids trying to sneak out past curfew. But that meant there were fewer things to crash into, fewer abandoned cars blocking the way, and fewer unpredictable zombies (or whatever the hell they were) slamming themselves blindly against mailboxes and light posts.

They were all silent for a stretch, save the rhythmic groan of the truck and Carlos's murmured cursing from the back.

Tree limbs were everywhere, snapped clean and spiked in the ground like javelins. A picket fence looked flayed, wooden slats stripped clean but still speared through the dirt as though some great hand had plucked them out and flung them. A swingset dangled from a stop sign twenty feet up. No rain, but the world looked beaten down with the awkward chaos left by something that didn't care how much humans had tried to organize it.

The wind had finally died away completely during the short drive, but the sky still sulked with heavy bruised-colored clouds, the purples and yellows almost glowing with unnatural luminosity. Any trace of sunlight that might've hinted at normalcy was swallowed by that ceiling of smoke-hinted gray.

They turned off Mill River Road where the pavement buckled like someone had punched straight up from underground. The street to Hawthorne's neighborhood tightened with dense old oaks. Here and there, broken glass and patio chairs scattered across lawns hinted at lives mid-interruption. Curtains hung out half-split windows like tongues.

When they rolled into the driveway of Hawthorne's house, a small green craftsman-style home sandwiched between larger rentals, the front stoop was nearly hidden by the crumpled limb of what used to be the neighbor's magnolia tree. One shutter had peeled off and was leaning against the porch light. The steps up to the porch were barely visible.

The house had held.

"I don't see anything moving," Leo said carefully, still standing in the cab, peering through the windshield. "Except your flamingo."

In the tangled remains of garden and mulch, a single pink plastic flamingo valiantly stood where he had been planted, listing at an angle but otherwise untouched.

"No one messes with Larry," Hawthorne murmured. Her voice was dry, but her throat burned with worry.

Behind her, Rucha helped Carlos toward the cab. He was pale, but steady, with his arm and shoulder wrapped to hell and back with bandages.

"Used a wrap, gauze, gauze again, and a sports band from the merch drawer," she said proudly. "The one that says 'Taco the Town.'"

Carlos tried a smile. "Actually feels better than it did before. I think you literally held me together."

"I aim to please."

Hawthorne leaned out of the cab, eyeing the path to the front steps. There were signs of earlier movement, as if something had been dragged across the yard—but no visible bodies, no blood, no immediate horror. Just ruin and silence and a strangely watchful stillness, like the neighborhood was holding its breath.

"You two stay here," Hawthorne said, glancing over her shoulder at Rucha and Carlos. "Lock the doors as soon as we get out. If it gets bad again, drive around the block. Just keep moving."

Rucha gave a tight nod. "Ten minutes tops. If you're not back, we're sending in the flamingo."

Carlos let out a wheezing chuckle that turned into a cough. "Larry to the rescue."

Hawthorne hopped out first, boots hitting the cracked pavement. Leo followed less gracefully, stumbling a bit as he cleared the gap from cab to curb. They moved quickly, low, eyes scanning windows and trees for movement that never came.

She noticed his hand hovering near the small of her back, not to push or guide, but a silent sort of solidarity.

The front door came open easier than it should have. She'd locked it that morning, but she hadn't accounted for the frame warping slightly from the battering of the wind and rain. The deadbolt scraped, and then it clicked.

Inside the smell of lavender and potting soil and basil was comfortingly normal. The hanging drying racks hadn't moved, but several books lay scattered across the floor, fallen from their shelves. A broken vase made small, glittering danger in the hallway.

They stepped in like they were trespassing. The house felt unnaturally still, save for the thrum of adrenaline Hawthorne couldn't shake from her limbs. She moved toward the kitchen automatically and grabbed the biggest knife from the butcher block. Her mother's chef blade, weighted and sharp.

Leo didn't hesitate. He plucked the broom from behind the pantry door and held it like a dull, confused saber.

Hawthorne arched a brow.

He shrugged. "I make do."

They crept past the kitchen, past the room Hawthorne had once slept in before she moved into the guest room to give Marla the bigger room for her sewing projects, and then stopped outside the bathroom. The light beneath the door flickered like a candle flame. From inside came the dried rattle of an air purifier, a soft shush-hiss in rhythmic tones of Marla's comfort machine.

Hawthorne tapped the wood lightly with the handle of her knife.

"Mama?"

A pause, then, "Say something only my baby would know!"

Hawthorne blinked, then forced a smile. "You won the chili cook-off in '05 with dried porcini mushrooms and raw cocoa powder."

The lock turned and the door cracked open just enough for Marla's weathered face to poke through. Her eyes were alert and misty. "Damn right I did," she said, then pulled the door wide and engulfed Hawthorne in a hug that smelled like eucalyptus and floor cleaner.

They stood there for a moment, wrapped around each other like two halves of something barely held together. Then Marla pulled back to eye Leo skeptically over her glasses.

"And who's this tall drink of circumstance?" she asked.

He blinked. "Uh, Leo."

"Well, Leo, if you try anything funny, I'm still spry enough to jam this lavender air freshener up your nose."

"She's not exaggerating," Hawthorne warned flatly, stepping inside to take in the makeshift fortress.

Marla had indeed barricaded herself with towels, a jug of water, mason jars filled with cuttings, half a loaf of rustic bread, and what looked like dried lentils charging atop an old wireless hot plate. Myrtle, the peace lily, rocked gently near the toilet, alongside two succulents balanced inside a mixing bowl.

"You really planned for the siege, huh?" Hawthorne asked, voice thinning into a laugh.

"I was prepping for the apocalypse anyway," Marla said, gesturing broadly. "It just got here early and mixed up the script."

"You good to move?" Leo asked. He wasn't impatient, but there was a brittle edge in his tone that said they couldn't linger.

Marla nodded, stretching her back with a crackle of joints. "Give me a second to kiss Myrtle goodbye and I'll grab my go-bag."

"You have a go-bag?" Leo asked in half disbelief, half admiration.

"She really does," Hawthorne said with resignation. She had lived with her parents' mild paranoia about "nuclear winter" her whole life.

"Bug-out essentials," Marla said over her shoulder, already disappearing down the hall with a wink at Hawthorne. "You know I live with that new-age prepper podcast in my earbuds. Now it's time to earn my five-star fan rating!"

Hawthorne turned to Leo, who hadn't moved. He was staring back toward the front door.

"What?" she asked quietly.

He shook his head. "Just listening. Still quiet."

"Gonna thank me for being right yet?"

Leo glanced at her and *almost* smiled. "Not yet. But I will say you drive like you've tangled with the devil before."

"He wasn't ready for a three-point turn." She turned to her mother with a smirk, who had reappeared in the hallway with several bags slung over her shoulders and back, and dragging a rolling suitcase.

"My baby-bug learned to drive from her daddy. He was a former drag racer. She never misses!"

Hawthorne paused, fingers flexing on the knife's handle. The mention of her father made her realize that what came next was a choice they couldn't unmake.

They were safe for now, but that wouldn't last. The pounding on the truck, the aimless wandering outside, Frank (whatever he was now) all pointed to the fact that there was no way to know if the neighborhood would *stay* safe. If the things outside would leave them alone.

"Maybe we should stay here," she said quietly, more to herself than the others. "At least for a day. Catch our breath. It held through the storm."

Leo, who'd been scanning each window with the same intensity as a soldier, turned. "It's not secure enough. Too many windows, too many entrances. You've got four walls and a wish."

"But it's home..." Her voice trailed off.

Marla shifted her floral-patterned hiking backpack stuffed to the seams and gave Hawthorne an expression that brooked no argument. "Baby-bug, it's not about a building. It's about surviving long enough to find one again." Then, gesturing with one weathered hand, "The buffet off 81—the old New Times place—it's already boarded up. Big kitchen, thick walls, and rooftop access if we need a lookout or an exit."

Leo made a noise deep in his throat. "The buffet? Seriously? It's wide open on all sides. You want visibility. Sight lines. I work at the Hayden agri center, which has underground storage, solar panels, and it's already fenced. People are probably already setting up there."

"You say 'solar panels,' but the grid still works," Marla snorted. "My best friend's church used the old buffet building during the flood of 2018. It's on top of a hill. They had over seventy people in there and not a single case of trench foot."

"Trench—why is that your bar?" Leo stared at her in astonishment.

Hawthorne stepped between them, raising her hands. "Okay, okay, stop. We don't have time for a turf war between apocalypse ideals. The truck's secure, Rucha and Carlos are waiting, and whatever Frank turned into might have friends. We stay or we go."

Leo exhaled through his nose. "Fine. Majority rules?"

Marla crossed her arms. "You got any votes in your pocket, boy?"

Hawthorne rubbed her temples. "Look, the agri center makes sense for long-term supplies," she said slowly, weighing each word as if it might catch fire. "That's where people might be holed up."

Leo nodded, hopeful. "Exactly. It's a rally point if there is one, especially in the heart of the Calloway-Hayden campus."

"But the distance," Marla countered. "You saw that chaos. How many of those clangy, foot-dragging folks you figure are scattered between here and the agri center? What happens if the truck goes dead halfway? We're stranded in a cow field with no cover."

"So we hole up in an abandoned restaurant with the rats?" Leo's voice wavered somewhere between sarcasm and frustration.

"And what happens if there are already survivors there?" Marla said, ignoring him. "People get mean when resources are low. Your fences won't keep out bullets."

The horn blasted once, sharp, shrill, and unmistakably urgent.

Everyone froze.

Hawthorne's breath caught like a thread tangled in her throat.

Then another honk. This one longer, insistent.

"Shit." Leo was already moving, turning for the door, broom still in hand.

"Rucha wouldn't honk unless—" Hawthorne didn't bother finishing the sentence. She dashed after him, Marla on her heels, go-bags jostling against her hips. Hawthorne stopped long enough to grab the handle of the suitcase to carry it along.

Outside the house, the entire street looked like it was swallowed by dusk and storm murk despite the fact it was no later than 2:00 pm, and all at once Hawthorne felt like every shadow was hiding another zombie, another twisted figure just out of frame.

They reached the driveway just as Rucha threw open the service window of the truck.

Her eyes landed on them with raw relief. "Movement," she shouted across the shallow yard. "Three—I think three—coming from the east! Slow, but steady. You need to get in. Now!"

Carlos emerged behind her, pale but upright, clutching a spray bottle of cleaning vinegar like a grenade.

Hawthorne grabbed Marla's hand. "We've got to go. We can argue over salad bars and solar panels later."

"Fine by me," Marla huffed. "I've long since accepted that my golden years are gonna be mostly snack-based and on wheels."

Leo yanked open the truck's rear hatch and waved them in. Hawthorne boosted her mother up first, then scrambled in, kicking her legs up just as a low chorus of sounds echoed from a block away, unmistakably feet dragging, glass crunching under things that hadn't learned how to lift their soles.

Inside, the air was thick again with old fryer oil, blood, and nerves, but at least it was shared.

Leo shut the hatch behind them with a slam and turned toward Hawthorne. "Where to?"

She looked past him, out the windshield.

Their choices forked ahead: one way to the edge of town and open fields, the Hayden agri center glinting somewhere beyond in remembered theory, and the other toward the shell of an old buffet, boarded up and browned at the corners with time, but solid and centralized.

She climbed into the driver's seat and cranked the engine. "Mom, I hate to disagree, but a rotting old buffet isn't a good base for us."

Her mother looked at her from where she had set her backpack down on a prep counter. Carlos and Rucha looked at each other in confusion.

She met her mother's incredulous stare. "It's not about comfort or location anymore. The agri center has power, food reserves, sustainability. Based on what we've seen, the whole region was likely knocked out by that freaky storm. So it will be days before the National Guard shows up, if not a week or more. FEMA even longer. Right now, everything is about holding out for the long term."

Marla gave a tight-lipped nod, folding her arms over her chest. "Fine. But I swear to every elder in my gardening club, if some canned-bean prepper tries to ration me out of my chamomile tea—"

"We'll start a revolution," Rucha said, grinning faintly as she reached for the chicken-wire hook that used to hold their apron smocks and now served as a makeshift IV loop for her water bottle. "Or a tea party. Either way, I'm in."

Carlos groaned from his perch near the back counter, offering Rucha a thumbs up. "No bad tea. That's the new law."

"And no trench foot," Leo added with a wry look at Marla.

Hawthorne smiled despite herself, dropping the van into reverse. The tires wriggled, then caught, scraping over the cracked driveway where magnolia bark still clung to manhole covers. She eased the truck out, swerving wide to avoid a twisted hunk of fence post—and took one final look at her house.

The curtains inside still moved, trickled by draft or memory. As if they were softly waving goodbye.

Not goodbye, she thought with a determined breath, but *see you later*. Once the world stopped being cursed, she would come back.

"Grid's still functioning," Leo murmured from the front, peering at the blinking red hand of a pedestrian crossing sign. "Streetlights are working if they're not knocked over. That's good."

Rucha shook her phone at them. "GPS? Down. Can't get to any of my websites, but I've been texting with my brother. He and the rest of my family are holed up at the hotel. But when I tried to call it wouldn't go through."

"I can't get through to my parents at all, text or chat," Carlos said, holding his own phone. "But then, they are in Kansas."

Hawthorne's fingers tightened on the wheel. "We have to assume things are going to stop working at some point."

"Cheery," Rucha muttered behind her, then added, "But she has a point."

Carlos chuckled weakly, rubbing his bandaged shoulder. "I don't care where we go as long as there's somewhere to sit and not die for a while."

Marla nodded solemnly. "We're gonna get you some soup the first chance we get. Soup solves more than people give it credit for."

A quiet beat passed as Hawthorne turned a corner onto the southbound street, driving at half-speed, careful to avoid tree limbs, debris, and the occasional vehicle half-draped in garden netting or trash bags like improvised armor.

"You all notice there aren't any bodies around?" Rucha asked, squinting out the window around Leo, who remained standing next to the driver's seat. "Yeah," Hawthorne replied, frowning. "There were people. Lots of them. Screaming, running, then just gone. Like the whole town folded in on itself."

Marla tilted her head. "You think they got out?"

"Wouldn't there be wrecks?" Rucha said. She leaned closer to the window. "Car doors left swinging open, bags left behind, piles of stuff? Something?"

Carlos gave a soft exhale that might've been a laugh. "Maybe they all turned. Just dropped right in place, stood up again wrong."

Everyone went quiet.

"Or it's the rapture and we're the sinners who got left behind?" Rucha chirped with forced cheer.

"Impossible," Hawthorne said, knowing she was right.

"Why's that?" Leo asked with a curious smirk. She willed her heart not to flutter, she had more important things to focus on, like street debris.

"Mom's still here. She's a saint. If the good people were taken up, she'd be one of the first," Hawthorne said simply because it was true.

"Hawthorne," her mother softly complained from the back, but it sounded like she was smiling.

Leo cleared his throat. "We don't know anything for fact yet and shouldn't make assumptions yet."

"That said, it feels like something's missing," Hawthorne said, eyes flicking across the empty sidewalks, the dark windows. "Even if people ran. There'd be more litter, more chaos left behind. There are too many cars just sitting around empty."

"I always thought the world ending would be louder," Carlos murmured.

"That weird storm was plenty loud," Hawthorne said with a shrug. "It's the *now* that's all quiet."

Marla huffed. "See, that's the apocalypse trap. Everyone thinks it'll be thunder and fire for days, but it's the quiet that'll kill you. The sudden space where noise used to be."

Hawthorne turned onto Meadow Street, close enough now to see the university's outer edges. The administration building loomed dark and silent, no movement in the windows. No mobs. No crowds.

It should've been comforting.

It wasn't.

"If the agri center's anything like the main campus," Leo said, folding his arms, "we're walking into a cathedral of ghosts."

"Oh, you're a poetic one, aren't you?" Marla marveled.

"That'll make it easier to pick a bunk," Carlos quipped.

Rucha snorted, then rubbed her eyes. "I vote no haylofts. Pretty sure my allergies would kill me faster than the zombies."

"They're not *zombies*," Leo said automatically, obviously too tired to push it but too stubborn to let it go.

"They're not *not* zombies," Hawthorne muttered under her breath. Then louder, "We're almost there. Should be another block, then the service road."

Up ahead, the tall fencing around the agri center, originally designed to keep out local wildlife and drunk undergrads, quietly loomed. They finally rolled to a slow stop in front of the agri center's main gate.

The tires groaned as Hawthorne eased down on the brake, and the truck hissed faintly like it was sighing with them. The gate was ten feet of cross-hatched metal and reinforced mesh that was shut tight and appeared untouched by the storm. Not even a dent.

For the first time since they'd gotten on the road, Hawthorne felt something snarl in her stomach. The sight of that gate, so solid and expressionless, made her hands twitch on the steering wheel.

Leo stepped forward, brushing past her knee to reach the dash. "I work here, remember? I've got an access card," he said, digging into the front pouch of his jacket. "Give me a second and I'll pop it open."

"Wait," Hawthorne said, suddenly tense. "What if there's someone inside already?"

"Even better." Leo clenched the card between his fingers. "They'll let us in."

He turned for the door, but before he reached the latch, a figure stepped into view on the other side of the gate.

She was short and stocky with dark olive skin and military-straight posture. Her salt-and-pepper hair was tied tight and frizzing at the corners from humidity. A long green duster coat flared slightly as she adjusted the weight of the open shotgun slung over one shoulder. She didn't move aggressively but she stood with the quiet confidence of someone who didn't need to.

"Well," Leo muttered. "Guess I don't need the card."

Hawthorne narrowed her eyes through the windshield. "You know her?"

"Yeah," he breathed. "That's Dr. Rachel Mendez." He reached for the door. "She is the director of the agri center."

On the other side of the gate, Dr. Mendez lifted the shotgun and snapped it close, letting it rest in her hold, aimed at the ground but an obvious, pointed symbol.

Then she called out, loud and unmistakably firm.

"Y'all better not be one of the dead ones."

Leo pushed the door open and stepped out.

CHAPTER 4

The Hayden Agri Center

There was something oddly reassuring about the way Dr. Mendez slung the cracked shotgun over one arm like it was just another garden tool instead of a loaded weapon. Hawthorne watched her unlock the main gate with swift, practiced movements, no nerves, no hesitation, just a commanding kind of calm that settled over every move she made.

"You're lucky I'm on gate duty; Eli has a twitchy finger right now," Dr. Mendez said, swinging the gate open with a high-pitched screech of metal. She stepped aside with a nod to Leo, eyes scanning the rest of them as Hawthorne pushed the truck forward through the entrance.

Leo gave her a sharp, tired nod. "I figured you'd still be holding it down."

"And I figured if I stared long enough down University Avenue, something would come crawling up it, stupid and loud." She jerked her chin at the truck. "Looks like I was half-right."

Rucha leaned out the side window. "Hey now, we might be stupid, but we bring the spice!"

Dr. Mendez snorted but didn't argue. She slammed the gate shut behind the last wheel, snapped the lock into place, then rapped twice on the steel with the back of her hand, obviously some kind of habit that struck Hawthorne as militaristic in nature.

Then the quiet returned, broken only by the faint pop of the truck's engine cooling.

With a start, Hawthorne realized that they had made it to *safety*.

The agri center stretched before them like the aftermath of a dream Hawthorne only half-remembered: the low-slung greenhouses, enormous and speckled with water from the storm, glinting against the late-afternoon sun; massive planting bed with rows of leafy green stalks in tight loamy beds around them, the soil dark and rich. The scent of compost wafted faintly through the air.

But it was the silence that hit hardest.

She had expected people. Dozens or more. *Hundreds* more. Students, faculty, staff…

Instead, there were only three hovering under the awning of the closest building—a tall white guy with forestry boots and wide shoulders, a young woman with a ponytail and a clipboard, and a girl who couldn't have been more than eighteen, curled up on a bench wearing a hoodie emblazoned with "Calloway-Hayden University of Agriculture & Mechanical Arts" which was about four sizes too big.

That was it.

Five survivors. Six if you counted Hawthorne.

Seven with Carlos, who barely managed to sit upright. Eight with Rucha. Nine with Marla.

"Where is everybody?" she demanded as she stumbled out of the truck.

Dr. Mendez raised a brow at Hawthorne's question, but her tone remained steady, as though the apocalypse were just an inconvenient thunderstorm she'd been asked to work around.

"Inside," she said, stepping back as if that answered everything. "Most of them, anyway. We've been reinforcing the perimeter access on all the external-facing buildings since the storm cleared. We've just started but my plan is to board up weak entry points, rerouting traffic through a single funnel gate. From what I've seen, the zombies aren't smart enough to open a door, but a panicked survivor running from them might leave one open."

Leo had already moved to the front of the truck, shaking out his arms like they'd gone numb from tension. "How many came in before us?"

Dr. Mendez finally offered a flicker of emotion, a crease of tired relief tucked into a nod. "First wave was about sixty, mostly students, some staff. Then a trickle of folks from the community, a few faculty families. Including those already in the center, last we counted: one hundred and ninety-seven, not including you five."

Hawthorne blinked. Her knees briefly wobbled with the weight of that number. It was both more and less than she'd expected. One hundred and ninety-seven should feel like a crowd.

It didn't.

Dr. Mendez gestured for them to follow and turned, her broad figure cutting a confident path toward the closest building, where the other three were still waiting. As they walked, Carlos leaned a little too hard on Rucha's side, and she cinched her arm around him, keeping him upright with sheer force of personality.

The gravel crunch beneath their boots, reminding Hawthorne that the last time she had walked this path, she'd been tagging along with her dad for a lecture, eager and naively confident, years before anything in her life required triaging.

Now, dried blood crusted her forearm where it had been missed during her desperate cleanup. Her stomach roiled.

"Everyone accounted for?" Leo asked quietly, falling into step beside Dr. Mendez.

She paused just long enough to squeeze the bridge of her nose. "No. We've got a rough roster. Still missing maybe twenty-five staff and students I know should've made it here by now. We had to clear out about fifty of those...things." She paused. "Dr. Hilfinger." She glanced out of the side of her eye at Leo, who scrunched up his face.

"Not a popular guy?" Hawthorne asked.

"No." Dr. Mendez shook her head. "But why did you ask?"

Hawthorne exchanged a look with Rucha before answering. "Our boss was a real jackass. Micromanager, arrogant, incompetent, the whole shebang. We watched him turn into a zombie when the storm came through."

Dr. Mendez snorted. "Sounds like Daryl, except he managed to be all that while also calling my soil rotation model 'sweetly ambitious.'" Her lip curled slightly. "If he turned, at least he's finally contributing to the ecosystem."

Leo and Carlos both made noises between a cough and a grim chuckle, and for a split-second, the tension around all of them fuzzed at the edges. But it didn't last.

"Seems like the zombie curse has a type," Hawthorne said, putting it together as she talked.

"It's a 'zombie curse,' huh? Interesting idea." Mendez squinted into the horizon.

"Does anything else make sense? I mean even pandemics have load times. This was *boom shakalaka boom* and now Frank's a zombie," Rucha spoke expressively with her hands flying through the air, possibly trying to imitate lightening. Hawthorne giggled and slapped a hand over her mouth.

With a sigh, Leo rolled his shoulders once, then turned toward Dr. Mendez and gestured behind him.

"Mendez, this is Hawthorne Porter," he said first, voice even but still wary. "She's the one who drove us here through whatever that was."

Dr. Mendez's eyes flicked to Hawthorne, sharp and thoughtful, reading deep. "You work for the food truck?" she guessed.

Hawthorne forced a smile. "Yeah. Head chef. And yes, I also have a commercial driving license."

"Good," Mendez said, not bothering with a smile. "We're short on useful skills. Glad to have you."

Leo went on. "This is Rucha who works with Hawthorne. Kept a level head and apparently doubles as a field medic when needed."

Rucha gave a little wave. "I do what I can. We also brought herbs."

Mendez raised an eyebrow. "Culinary or...?"

"Little of column A, little of B," Rucha replied cheerfully. "Always helps to be versatile."

Leo didn't even flinch, just shifted and gestured toward Carlos, now hunched over slightly but still standing with dogged effort. "Carlos got swiped bad fighting off Hawthorne's boss, but he's stable.

"Glad you made it, Carlos. We'll get you looked after properly. Any fever?"

"Not yet," he said. "Just sore. Thanks, Dr. Mendez."

Dr. Mendez nodded once, then finally turned to the last member of the team.

Leo stepped aside slightly so Marla could move into better view. Her patchwork backpack gave her the look of someone either heading to a farmer's market or preparing to charm woodland spirits into revealing their secrets.

"This is Marla Porter," he said carefully. "Hawthorne's mom. She managed to hold her position during the storm. Locked herself in a bathroom."

Marla offered a hand to Dr. Mendez with a breezy smile. "I also brought emotional stability and several thriving succulents. Pleasure to meet you, Doc."

Dr. Mendez looked at the offered handshake like it was something unusual, then seemed to decide she liked it. Her palm met Marla's in a firm grip. "Glad to have another adult in the room. Most people under forty are wild-eyed and halfway to bad decision-making."

Marla chuckled, eyes twinkling. "Oh, I specialize in bad decisions. But I dress them up chamomile and honey."

At that, Dr. Mendez gave something suspiciously close to a smirk. "Noted."

Hawthorne groaned softly, dragging her palm across her face before hissing at her mother. "Can you not? Just for... five minutes?"

"Don't be jealous, baby-bug," Marla said, gazing innocently at the sky. "Some people just vibe."

"She say 'baby-bug'?" Mendez asked dryly.

"No." Hawthorne turned away before one of them could toss out another nickname like it was a grenade.

Leo cleared his throat, but his mouth twitched like he might laugh. "Anyway, that's all of us."

"Well," Dr. Mendez said, motioning toward the building, "we've got a medical student checking everyone for wounds or fever—room 104, just past soil analysis. And you'll get assigned a temporary bed by the end of the night. The agricultural center here doesn't have dorms so beds might be couches or rubber mats."

Hawthorne nodded, relief washing over her in a strange, unsteady wave. It wasn't a long-term solution, but it was solid ground. A place to breathe.

"I'll walk you in," Mendez added, then waved over the other three people.

Mendez jerked her chin to the trio hovering under the awning. "These three are part of the interim operations crew. Come meet the welcoming committee."

First to step forward was the tall man in the forestry boots, his bulk moving with surprising grace for someone who looked capable of wrestling a bear and winning on attitude alone. His face was all sharp lines and solemn silence, but Leo nodded like they knew each other already.

"This is Eli Dale," Mendez said. "Forestry grad student and former park ranger. Knows his way around a perimeter and the business end of an axe."

Eli gave a short, respectful nod. His eyes flicked from Hawthorne to the truck, to the bloodied edge of her shirt from earlier. "Glad you made it," he said, voice deep gravel over smooth stone. "Heard the truck. Figured that was either food or a disaster."

"Both," Rucha mumbled.

Leo grinned faintly. "Eli and I worked on the same soil sample collection camping trip last semester. He was in charge of not getting us lost in the woods, which he accomplished with minimal injuries."

"I don't get lost," Eli said without humor.

"Not what I heard," Carlos whispered behind Hawthorne.

Mendez waved them along as the clipboard-holding young woman stepped in next. Late twenties, maybe, with a swirl of messy curls forced back into a bun, and a pen clutched like it might fend off gremlins. She wore two nametags layered over each other, one handwritten and misspelled, the other scratched half-off by what looked a dried out eraser.

"This is Shelly," Mendez said. "She's my grad assistant and I've put her in charge of supplies, for now."

"Tryin' my best," Shelly said with a weary but anxious shrug. "There's a ledger system. Or there was. Mostly. You'll see the signs. There are color codes. Don't ask what green labels mean." She stopped, visibly rebooted her social instincts, and offered Hawthorne a shaky smile. "Nice to meet you. Sorry. Kind of lost my filter somewhere about two hours ago."

Hawthorne blinked but smiled back. "It's okay. I tried to kill my boss. We're all adapting."

At the word "kill," Shelly turned an interesting shade between peach and grey. "I... okay, good start," she stammered. Then she scribbled something—possibly a reminder to avoid the food truck for a while.

Finally, the girl in the oversized hoodie looked up from where she'd been bouncing one leg a little too fast. The tips of her box braids were dyed a fading magenta. Stickers lined her water bottle, all horticulture club jokes and "protect native plant species" slogans.

Dr. Mendez tilted her head toward her. "And that's Maggie. Undergraduate in the agriculture program. She's our runner—delivers messages, urgent supplies, morale stickers, whatever needs moving between teams."

The girl perked up at her name and grinned. "Hey, Dr. Foxx. Didn't think a tenured future would require the 'survive zombies' module, huh?"

Leo sighed. "It was an optional unit. Clearly, you did the reading."

Maggie brightened. "Only because your office has the emergency snacks."

"And because you're afraid of worms," Carlos added, recovering enough strength to lean against the wall.

"I'm not afraid of worms," Maggie shot back. "I just don't like how they move. It's weird."

"I kind of get that," Hawthorne muttered before she could stop herself. "Like very tiny accordion players out for vengeance."

Now it was Rucha's turn to snort into her palm from behind Carlos.

Mendez held up both her hands, flattening the chaos. "Enough. We get more introductions later, after you've all been checked out by Jake in Medical."

Hawthorne glanced over at Leo, whose face was still tight beneath the deflecting quips and tired observations. She brushed a hand against the hem of her shirt and realized, with a dull flash of surprise, that her hands no longer felt sticky.

They weren't clean yet, but they felt steady again.

As they reached the front of the research building, Dr. Mendez moved with more purpose. She passed the shotgun off to Eli and started writing on a clipboard that had appeared like magic from under her coat. "In the past hour, we've cleared the main buildings. The admin offices in Hotcher will be our dorms, plenty of privacy and restrooms for everyone. Triage is here in the south wing, ground floor, next to the old test kitchen and lab."

Hawthorne perked up slightly. "You've got a kitchen?"

"We've got two. Converted the soil testing bay to an outdoor test kitchen a few years ago," she replied without missing a beat. "It survived the storm just fine." She glanced over at Leo. "From what we can tell so far, the greenhouses weren't damaged, miraculously. Harshest thing out here right now's the smell of sprouted lentils."

Marla looked suddenly intrigued. "Sprouted lentils, huh? How's morale with those on the menu?"

"We instituted sarcasm as currency," Dr. Mendez said. "It's going well."

They filed inside the building, which had a large sign reading "E. Delacroix Agricultural Sciences Center," and Hawthorne felt the temperature shift, the cool calm of a building designed to protect fragile plants and expensive chemicals providing a strange sort of comfort.

They passed a few people carting crates, others hammering nails into stacked tables used as window-barriers. No one shouted. No one panicked. Everyone moved with quiet routine, the way you only got if someone had told them what to do and made it stick. Hawthorne assumed that someone was Dr. Mendez.

"Give me five minutes with those doing a perimeter check," Dr. Mendez said to Leo, turning at the split in the corridor. "Get settled. I'll circle back."

Leo nodded once, formally. For once, there was no teasing in his tone, only a professional kind of gravity. "Appreciate it, Dr. Mendez."

Eli, Shelly, and Maggie peeled off behind Dr. Mendez with no more discussion, their footsteps receding into one of the side corridors. The heavy click of Eli's boots was the last to vanish. Hawthorne couldn't help but notice that even Maggie, who had the slight bounce of someone running on breakfast sugar and not much else, snapped into clean, purposeful motion when the doctor gave orders. Whatever else Mendez was—stern, weapon-hoisting, gravel-dry—she had gravity.

Leo steered them down the left hallway, past a row of classroom-style labs that now doubled as triage zones, until they reached the door marked "Supply." A taped-on handwritten sign underneath read: TEMPORARY E.R. - PLEASE DO NOT SCREAM. WE'RE ALL DOING OUR BEST.

Inside the room, which looked like an old classroom converted to storage, the overhead fluorescents flickered but held steady. The shelving along the walls was crammed full of random stuff, including canned food, bags of dried beans, reams of printer paper, boxes labeled "unused sample kits," and bins of various sizes of plastic trash bags.

A row of cot mats lined the wall, each one topped with folded scratchy gray blankets and a roll of gauze tucked by the corner like a hotel chocolate. Two wide folding tables were stacked with antiseptic bottles, first-aid packs, protein bars, and boxes of disposable gloves.

"Take a seat, Carlos," Leo said gently, gesturing toward the nearest cot. "Jake should be here in a second to check you out. He's technically pre-med, but he knows what he's doing. Or close enough to bluff it."

Carlos obediently went over and parked himself with a relieved grunt. "As long as nobody tries leeches," he said, easing down like a man twice his age.

As Rucha hovered nearby, readjusting his bandages for the third time, Marla began to pace a slow circle around the supply shelves, her hands trailing gently over labeled bins as she scanned everything like a hungry ghost at a library buffet.

"Y'all have a decent cache here." she murmured. "But it won't last forever. We'll need to ration."

"We haven't even settled down yet and you're already worried about rationing?" Rucha asked, slightly incredulous. She perched herself on a stool next to Carlos and kicked one boot rhythmically against the side of it.

Marla didn't turn around. "That's how we stretch what matters. Don't wait for the scarcity to start before acting like it's here."

Carlos frowned. "You're acting like we'll be camped out here for weeks. The National Guard should be showing up soon."

Marla finally turned to face them, crossing her arms over her chest, brows lifting in quiet judgment. "You expect the cavalry to roll through tomorrow with hot towels and warm soup?"

Hawthorne raised a hand, palm up. "The internet is down, sure, but we still have power. The grid's up. Streetlights and signage were working the whole drive back. Communications are damaged but calls and texts are getting through," she said.

"True. I just got a text from our youngest brother, he's locking up the pool at the hotel," Rucha agreed, holding up her phone.

"Yeah, but I can't get through to my folks in Kansas." Carlos did not look very upset about that, but Hawthorne knew better than to press.

Leo nodded, arms folded loosely as he leaned against the shelf opposite Marla. "There's been no official evac, no national alert, no push notifications. Feels wrong, but not permanent. Just... glitching."

Carlos gestured with his good arm. "Okay, but let's say the storm knocked out comms, maybe local towers or whatever. Why aren't the National Guard crawling all over the highways by now?"

"There weren't even helicopters," Hawthorne said suddenly as the realization hit her. "I didn't see a single damn chopper in the air. You're telling me something like this happens and not one guy in a headset calls in an aerial flyover? You ever seen weird green storms roll in somewhere and not get weather-nerd drones for days?"

Marla leaned against the wall and tilted her chin, half-amused. "You know what they say about logical observations in a catastrophe?" She paused. "No one wants them."

"That's... not super comforting, Mom," Hawthorne muttered.

"It's gotta be a regional event," Leo said quietly. His stare was steady but uncertain in the corners. "No way the whole country just failed overnight without a single whisper."

"Then where are the people?" Marla asked, voice soft now, not accusatory. "We drove fifteen blocks and saw more trees than humans.

And not a single emergency barricade. Not even one flipped siren car. No messed-up news vans... nothing."

They all fell into a heavy quiet, the kind that always followed when someone asked a question nobody wanted to answer.

After a moment, Rucha cleared her throat and tried for a smile. "Okay, so. Our options are: terrifying silence is good, terrifying silence is bad, or terrifying silence is an elaborate prank setup from a rival university's ag department."

Hawthorne chuckled weakly. "Swamp monsters with a grudge."

Marla sighed and walked over to the oversized calendar whiteboard near the supply room entrance, which was mostly blank, save for a curved scribble that read "supply-inventory—ask Shelly."

"We *assume* this is temporary," she said, tapping twice on the edge of the board with her fingernail. "But I think we need to plan for the long haul, just in case. That way, either we're ready or we get pleasantly surprised when someone in uniform knocks on the gate with hot coffee and FEMA."

"Optimism through preparedness?" Leo asked with a slight smirk, which made him devilishly handsome. Hawthorne had to look away.

"It's what your daddy used to say," Marla added with a sad little shrug in Hawthorne's direction. "Right after he installed rain barrels and tried to build a cold smoker entirely out of car parts."

"I'm still mad he never finished that project," Hawthorne muttered, then caught herself smiling.

"Wait, hold up. What's a cold smoker?" asked Rucha from where she was reorganizing a box of medical bandages. "Is that like, smoked tofu? Smoked sushi?"

"Both," Marla and Hawthorne said in unison, then grinned at each other with identical quirked eyebrows.

"Once you smoke fish it's not sushi anymore." Rucha finally sat down next to Carlos.

Leo stood up straight, the weight in his shoulders loosening just enough for Hawthorne to see past the academic or the ad hoc emergency strategist. He nodded toward the room. "Well... welcome to the new normal, I guess. At least for now."

Carlos huffed at that. "I swear, if zombie-pocalypse leadership gets restructured based on culinary performance, I want it on the record that my loyalty lies with the tofu grinder goddess."

Rucha raised her hand. "Seconded."

Marla raised both hands. "And my child's kitchen knife technique is an extension of divine will."

"That's three votes," Rucha said, turning toward Hawthorne with a smirk. "Guess you're president now."

Hawthorne blinked at them, caught unnervingly between laughter and actual nausea. "Oh God. If I'm in charge of feeding all of you, I'm gonna need more than three sprigs of curling rosemary and a bag of apocalypse beans."

"Then maybe stay close to the greenhouse," Leo offered, teasing just under the surface, and then his gaze softened. "We'll make it work."

Hawthorne looked around at her strange, lurching group of survivors.

She hadn't planned this.

She hadn't planned to kill her boss, either. Or flee across a city swallowed by a supernatural storm. She hadn't planned to drive her mother away from their home to a place she barely remembered from field trips and lazy spring lectures, and she definitely hadn't planned to be surrounded by people who suddenly—strangely—expected her to keep them sane, fed, and moving forward.

But here they all were, somehow orbiting around her.

She looked at Leo again, caught the quiet steadiness sitting behind his eyes—not the kind of calm that asked to be followed, but the kind that steadied your hand when you were already running. And she thought: maybe we're more ready than we feel.

Hawthorne tilted her head back against the wall and let the moment settle, quiet around the edges, absurd in the middle. Out the narrow glass window, she could see the edge of the greenhouse beginning to gleam gold again, sunset pouring through the panels like the world itself was sighing.

Safe. For now.

"You think we'll still be here tomorrow?" she asked without meaning to, her voice smaller than it had sounded before the day began.

"Yeah," Leo answered, quick and firm.

Hawthorne didn't answer. She just let her eyes close for a breath or two. "I guess I need to figure out how to feed two hundred people on the fly."

Leo chuckled softly. "At least for now."

She glanced at him. "Do you really think the National Guard will show up soon?"

He grimaced. "I like to believe it's a strong possibility, but your mother isn't wrong in allowing for the fact they might take a while to get here. Whatever that storm was, it probably took out chunks of infrastructure across the whole region. That's not even counting the damn zombies." He sighed, then added, softer: "But I think we'll still be standing, too."

"You're right. They take a while when it's just a local catastrophe. They might be busy with the big cities right now." She instinctively looked up, her mother's words haunting her.

"Someone hurt?" A short blond guy stumbled into the room. "I'm Jake, med school student and EMT trainee!" He stopped and looked around, eyes falling on Carlos. "Oh, yeah, okay." He dashed forward and started undoing all the bandaging. Rucha got up somewhat reluctantly and shuffled close to Marla, who had sat down with her bags on one of the cots.

Hawthorne's nerves were shot and she kind of wished they were in the middle of lunch rush or something, not sitting around watching Carlos get repaired.

Then she stood up straight. "Rucha!" she called out across the room.

Rucha glanced up. "Did I get promoted or fired? I wasn't listening."

Hawthorne strode over, tugging her ponytail tighter like it would keep her thoughts from unraveling. "We're finding the kitchen. You, me. We need eyes on what's actually here before I start creating menus out of thin air. And we have a lot of people to feed, at least for the next forty-eight hours. Maybe longer."

Rucha rubbed her hands together. "Finally. I've been dying to see what horrors await in the pantry of a university research center."

Marla arched a brow from her perch. "I'm assuming you're planning to coerce labor out of your immediate family?"

Hawthorne tossed her mother a look. "I'm planning to ask very nicely if you'd mind overseeing some inventory. Carlos can help you move things around once he's released from here." Unspoken would be that he would likely be carrying around a chair for her mother to sit in. Hawthorne could see the tight lines around her eyes that signified her arthritis was acting up.

Carlos raised his uninjured hand weakly. "Sounds like dangerous work. Where's my high-visibility vest?"

Marla made a show of stretching with a pained sound. "Fine. But I retain the right to critique your choice of spice categories."

"Do you even know what we have yet?" Hawthorne asked, half-laughing, half-panicked.

"My judgment does not require context." Marla hoisted herself up and gave Carlos a conspiratorial smile. "Meet me in the pantry later, handsome."

"Mom!" Hawthorne screeched while everyone laughed, even Jake.

Leo eased away from where he'd been watching. "I should check in with Mendez, see what her plans actually are."

"You sure?" Hawthorne asked. The idea of him stepping out again made something ripple beneath her ribs, but she stuffed it down.

He gave her a long look, something curved and quiet and weighty. "Yeah. You've got food to deal with, and I..." A faint smile. "I'll make sure the doors stay closed behind us."

She nodded, then something stubborn made her add, "Don't get heroic."

Leo's grin kicked up, tired but real. "I'm too tired to try to be a martyr."

With that, he slid out the door like a shadow against concrete, his footsteps steady and deliberate.

Rucha turned to Hawthorne as soon as he was gone. "So, kitchen?"

"Kitchen," Hawthorne confirmed. She glanced at the paper map taped to the wall—an outdated fire route plan with sticky notes and scribbles on it from years of students adding commentary, and some rooms changing purpose. She ran her finger along the corridor labels, scanning for the converted test kitchen Mendez had mentioned. South wing, ground floor. It was marked with two asterisks and a bolded note in red Sharpie that read: "Hot plates ONLY, Dave. This is why you're not allowed near the propane again."

"Dave must be fun at parties," Rucha muttered, peering over Hawthorne's shoulder.

"I don't think anybody's gonna be partying anytime soon," Hawthorne replied, then motioned. "Come on. This way."

They ducked out of the supply room and took the hallway back through the inner corridor, passing a tall student stacking empty seed trays and humming quietly under his breath who nodded politely at them as they walked by. The entire place smelled faintly of potting soil, mold-resistant caulk, and bleach.

The kitchen sat behind a set of double doors with ventilation fans mounted above them, barely humming. A laminated sign had been blotted partially black by time and sun: EXPERIMENTAL CULINARY LAB. Additional graffiti had been added in block letters: WHERE GOURMET GOES TO DIE.

Inside, it was a strange hybrid of industrial intentions and budget scraping—a long central counter divided by metal bins and rusted fixtures, rows of upper cabinets with mismatched handles, and two sinks that looked like they'd survived a burst pipe and a nervous breakdown. The old gas range was something out of a 1960s educational film. Someone had added a string of fairy lights over the cabinet labeled SPICES - SALT KEPT SEPARATELY IN CABINET R.

"And this," Rucha said dramatically, spinning once as she entered, "is my haunted kitchen dreamscape. God, this is fabulously tragic. It's like ye olde student struggle cave."

Hawthorne pulled open a cabinet and found rows of mismatched jars—some taped shut, some half-labeled, some clearly salvaged from multiple communal kitchens. She reached for one that said CORIANDER?? in Sharpie and shook it gently. The seeds inside made a faint, promising rattle, but they were indeed coriander.

"It'll do," she said under her breath. Then louder, "We'll start by cataloging what we have. Go through the dry goods and spices, label what's usable, what's spoiled, and whatever might be a choking hazard disguised as chickpeas." She looked over at a door temptingly labeled "Surplus," and pointed it out to Marla.

She saluted mockingly. "Captain of Provisions, reporting for pantry duty."

She walked toward the Surplus door with the dramatic gravity of someone leading an expedition to a haunted cave. Hawthorne and Rucha followed, pushing it open to reveal shelves upon shelves of bulk goods, emergency rations, dry mixes, canned vegetables, mystery bags of grain, and perhaps three lifetime supplies of instant mashed potatoes.

Rucha inhaled like they'd just found the Ark of the Covenant. "Oh ho. Look at this bounty of carbs!"

Hawthorne stepped forward, eyeing a dented can with a faded label that might have once said "kidney beans" or "congealed regret." Marla came up behind her.

"The vibe here is old and disorganized."

Rucha cracked her knuckles and pulled a small notepad from her coat pocket. "The vibe *and* the shelves. We will divide and conquer."

"Cool," Hawthorne replied. "You do that, I'm gonna check if that freezer is actually working or is just decorative."

As they began sorting—a rhythm of opening boxes, sniff tests, scribbled tallies, and Rucha's occasional outbursts like "What kind of monster stores dehydrated jalapeños next to the powdered milk?"—Carlos arrived with his arm in a sling. He stood in the doorway, face pale but amused.

"This humble post-doc is here to report for duty."

Marla yelled from deep in the supply room. "Humble's a stretch. But he does have nice shoulders."

"That's the arthritis talking," Rucha said, walking out of the pantry. "You're getting reckless with compliments."

"Nope, that's just me, hon."

Hawthorne ignored the ongoing exchange as Carlos switched places with Rucha, the two of them flirting in an extremely awkward way that Marla had very clear opinions about. Instead, Hawthorne crouched beside an open cabinet labeled UTENSILS—LARGE, like it was daring her to be disappointed.

Inside, there was a treasure trove of battered but beloved gear: industrial-sized stock pots stacked precariously like aluminum turtles, two cast-iron pans worn into something that looked like battlefield relics, and a massive mixing bowl that could double as a toddler-sized bathtub. She whistled low, dragging out the stock pot and checking its bottom for cracks. None. Just well-loved.

In the next large cabinet was a pressure cooker big enough to make stew for a football team or render an army of dried beans into submission. It bore a tag that read "Do NOT let Dr. Toby near this unsupervised" in furious black marker, which Hawthorne took as a sign of promise.

In the far back corner, tucked behind a rack of sheet trays and wire baskets, was an object she hadn't expected: a stainless steel smoker. Small for industrial use, but large enough to feed a dorm floor on a good day. She pulled off the canvas cover and let out an appreciative grunt. The power cord looked intact. The wood chip drawer still had shavings inside—applewood, maybe?

"That's not just a smoker," she murmured. "That's a morale machine."

Behind her, Rucha let out a yelp of triumph. "I have found twenty cans of fire-roasted tomatoes, sixteen full jars of veggie bouillon cubes, and—wait for it—a vacuum-sealed packet of saffron so old I think it predates ethics."

Carlos called from where he was now arranging dry goods in labeled bins, "You're hoarding the spice rack like a goblin!"

"Correction! I'm curating a legacy!"

Marla snorted appreciatively. "Let her have this moment, Carlos. If we're stuck eating sprouted lentils, we deserve at least one bite of flavor."

Hawthorne stood and surveyed the room again. It was set up like the first kitchen she had ever worked in, an old dorm on campus that served dozens of students for every meal. There was a dusty deep frier to one side, and the old gas stove had a huge griddle along with six burners. Some of the stove elements looked like they hadn't been used since the last time someone used a rotary phone. Still, it wasn't nothing.

"We can work with this," she muttered aloud. Then louder so that the others would hear: "Next big job is clearing out the walk-in. It's cold, so the power's holding, but we've got mystery meat labeled like a failed science experiment." She eyed the "cow test, 2/7/2017" with caution. "Remind me to ask Shelly to canvas for allergies!"

"Okay!" Rucha yelled back, obviously distracted—by inventory or Carlos, Hawthorne did not want to know.

Hawthorne rolled up her sleeves and stepped into the center of the kitchen like she belonged there. Because she did. Whatever else was happening in the world, she could work a kitchen.

She found a bin of long-grain rice in an old, plastic-lined, metal trash can in a small closet and hauled it back into the kitchen with a groan. Beside it, she placed a sack of orange lentils and a row of moderately dented coconut milk cans that smelled fine when opened. The ancient saffron packet, once Rucha had reverently placed it in her hands like a relic reclaimed from the ruins of flavor, sat proudly atop the cutting board like a crown.

"Alright," she said to the empty air and half-listening team mates. "Tonight, we're doing saffron lentil curry. It's simple, it's scalable, it's filling, and no one will complain because the alternative is instant mashed potatoes."

"Hallejujah!" Marla answered, muffled from somewhere deep in the storage shelves.

Hawthorne filled a huge stock pot with water and salt before getting it on the stove. The pilot light caught after the second match, and she grinned in a way that felt feral and victorious, like fire itself had agreed to not abandon her.

As the rice and lentils soaked in separate tubs, she checked supplies of onions, garlic, turmeric, and cumin. Not perfect, not her usual ingredients, but enough. The turmeric was clumpy, the onions sprouting slightly, and the cumin lived in a jar that had once held dried oregano, but that was fine. Improvisation was just the fancy chef word for panic with flair.

She recruited Rucha formally when the actual cooking started, because there was no way she could stir three industrial pots, taste for balance, and monitor boiling rice with only two arms and a rising sense of existential dread.

"I stir," Rucha said as she grabbed a battered wooden spoon nearly the length of her arm. "But I do so with *authority*."

"You stir," Hawthorne ordered, tossing split lentils into a second pot, "and you do it at medium heat or I banish you."

"Yes, ma'am," Rucha intoned solemnly.

Marla, from her new throne of a padded stool near the open storage shelves, offered quiet commentary and corrected their spice ratios with the delicate judgment of someone who had once believed the right seasoning could fix politics. Carlos shifted to sorting serving trays and laundered table linens at a folding table, flanked by two undergrads who'd wandered in looking for somewhere to be useful, although she suspected Leo had sent them.

Hawthorne wiped her palms on her apron, an oversized dish towel tied around her waist, and took a long breath as the aroma of toasted cumin and blooming garlic filled the air. For the first time in what felt like days, the scent didn't make her stomach clench in fear or nausea. It was warm and familiar and entirely human.

Outside the kitchen, the sky was shading into rust and violet. Through the grimy side windows, she could just make out flickers of movement from people running errands, carrying boxes of things to someplace or another, and for a strange moment, it was everything she'd ever wanted without knowing to ask: purpose, noise, good smells, a dozen tired people ready to do the meticulous, meaningful work of keeping each other alive.

She could hear Rucha humming off-key, the clink of ladles against industrial steel. Carlos was cracking jokes again, his voice still hoarse but stronger. Marla's laughter floated over it all like steam, familiar and impossible to ignore.

It wasn't normal—God, it was galaxies from normal—but it was something better than chaos. It was rhythm. People fitting into space together. She had missed that. And somehow so unexpectedly it made her chest ache, it was happening around her.

She didn't know how permanent it would be. Maybe they'd be rescued tomorrow. Maybe a whole military convoy would roll through and bring structure and neat little forms and warm meals none of them had to scrounge into existence. Maybe she'd go back to working for jerks like Frank for less money than she and Marla needed to live on.

She glanced around the kitchen, at her mother's joyful chaos, Carlos's understated confidence, and Rucha's dry one-liners as she worked with the undergrads to warm up tortillas pulled from the walk-in freezer on the griddle.

Hawthorne tasted the curry, adjusted the salt, and let the spoon linger for a breath longer than she needed to.

She liked being part of a team. She always had. It was why she always ended up working in kitchens, from the time she was old enough for her first job. She liked the way pieces came together when everyone offered something without having to be asked twice.

She also liked the feeling of being in charge—not *leading*, exactly, but anchoring. Feeding people was the oldest kind of magic, and she was good at it.

Turning around to her team, she put her hands on her hips. "Go let the masses know it's time to eat!"

CHAPTER 5
A Call to Action

Hawthorne stood before the simmering stock pot, hating the choices before her like a battlefield commander facing a losing battle.

The two dozen cracked eggs sat precariously in a metal bowl on the prep counter, looking pitiful, as if they knew they were nowhere near enough to feed nearly two hundred people.

She sighed and pushed her hair out of her eyes with the back of one hand. The patchy light filtering in through the east window glinted the top of the old, dinted industrial mixer and made the cracked tile floor look less grimy than it really was.

"Please don't hate me," she muttered aloud to the eggs, reaching for the rice slurry bubbling softly on the back burner. "It's not you. It's math."

She was already elbow-deep in congee prep, the rice already boiled past recognition into velvety oblivion—a childhood comfort she'd first learned to make from a friend's grandmother during a family trip to Houston, and one of the few things that made two grains of rice feel like a feast.

With a soft laugh to herself, she whisked the eggs into a golden frenzy. She moved the pot off the stove and slowly drizzled the mixture into the congee. Trails of hot yellow streaked through the pale porridge, oddly cheerful looking, she thought. Then she sprinkled in salt, soy sauce packets scavenged from a drawer in one of the breakrooms over in the Flores Research Facility, along with a heavy-handed pinch of white pepper and just enough powdered garlic to wake up a corpse.

Which she thought was maybe a little on the nose.

Voices hummed gently in the distance, from the long hallway beyond the kitchen where the dining area retrofit was well underway. The sound of hammering had quieted significantly, replaced by the softer shuffles of chairs, tables, and the warm undercurrent of people being... people.

The lecture hall that, Shelly told her, had once hosted guests speaking on microbial efficiency and community permaculture models —which she'd been informed everyone would listen to—was being turned into a makeshift dining room complete with folding tables, salvaged napkin dispensers, and twinkly string lights courtesy of someone's emergency camping kit.

Mendez's orders had come in late last night, sharp but thoughtful: "If we're staying, we eat together. If we eat together, we build community, and we're going to need to rely on each other for a while."

And her plan was working, at least in that subtle, aching way survival often did. At breakfast, people were going to sit down beside strangers and eat warm food with plastic spoons that would be diligently washed instead of thrown away, and then they would all get back to work.

She reached for a small bowl of scallions she'd sliced earlier. A quick sniff told her they were good quality with a snappy, clean, grass-bright odor. They had been pulled that very morning from one of the gardens by Carlos, who had given it like a flower bouquet to Rucha. She accepted it with uncharacteristic silence and a bright blush that Hawthorne was absolutely going to mock her for later.

She allowed herself a satisfied little hum as she divided the scallions, for topping the congee, into five small ramekins to be spread across the tables where people sat.

It wasn't the most glamorous meal, but it was a bowl of warmth that sat heavy in the belly and felt like something you'd find in the quiet of someone's childhood. That was the magic bit of it. Congee didn't need applause. It just needed a spoon and someone willing to take a bite and be surprised at how much it tastes like nostalgia.

Just as she nestled it into place on the long prep table, the door creaked open and Rucha slid inside. Her hair was up in a messy bun secured with what looked like a fork, and she had a clipboard balanced on her hip like a particularly sassy sword. "Dining hall retro-fit is officially ninety percent done," Rucha announced. "We have string lights, chalk-note table numbers, and one person—Jordan from admin—who volunteered to do stand-up comedy at each meal. I've already told him no six times.".

"Tell him seven," Hawthorne said, reaching for the box of mismatched spoons. "Nobody wants desperate Netflix special energy right now."

"Too late," Rucha said ominously. "He quoted Hannah Gadsby and someone clapped."

Hawthorne groaned. "He's going to get a cult."

"Probably," Rucha chirped, then drifted closer to sniff at the steaming pot of congee. "Ooooh, breakfast gruel. This looks... deceptively cozy."

"It is comfort incarnate," Hawthorne declared. "And we're stretching two dozen eggs across multiple meals for nearly two hundred people. Every micron of flavor is a tiny miracle. I even found chili oil packets."

Rucha leaned against the prep counter, arms crossed. "You are the single thread holding humanity together with scallions and a dream."

"Save the flirting for Carlos," Hawthorne said, laughing when Rucha's dusky skin turned dark with a blush.

"Shut up. I'm divorced and living in shame," she said, rolling her eyes.

"Carlos is cute enough that even your grandmother might forgive you," Hawthorne said in full honesty. Grandma Patel was one of the tiniest women she'd ever met, but while she ruled the family with an iron fist, she had a soft spot for Rucha. "Anyway, put out the small side bowls and coffee mugs. No one gets to hoard this. Small servings and then we'll see what's left."

Rucha dutifully grabbed stacks of mismatched bowls from the cabinets and began arranging them on a rolling cart like she was setting up for a very rustic bistro opening.

"I'm telling you," she said, pointing a spoon like a lecturing professor, "we need a chalkboard menu that changes daily. Every post-apocalyptic commune worth its salt ration has cute signage. I've seen the Pinterest pins."

"We have one dry erase marker," Hawthorne replied without looking up. "And it squeaks like a frightened mouse."

"That's the aesthetic," Rucha countered.

The door swung open again with a light squawk, and Leo stepped into the kitchen, his face flushed from the outdoors but his movements calm and steady. He had that not-quite-showered day-after disaster chic look most of them were sporting at that point, with a rolled-up flannel shirt and a tool belt slung diagonally across his narrow hips.

"Warm air, actual food, and petty arguments," he said dryly, stepping fully into the room. "Feels like home."

"Breakfast." Hawthorne motioned toward the massive pot.

Leo wandered over, peered into the pot, and made an impressed noise low in his throat. "Is that—seriously, congee?"

"Don't give me that look," she said. "You either trust me or you wake up to powdered eggs and regrets."

"I trust you," he said, without pause, then pulled out the small notepad tucked into the open pocket of his flannel. "Do we even have powdered eggs? Never mind. I came hunting you down to ask Rucha—any chance you've finished the pantry inventory?"

Rucha let out a long, beleaguered breath through her nose and waved her clipboard like it was a cursed scroll. "Finished? No. Alive and only mildly offended by cans of mangos in syrup that expired three presidential administrations ago? Yes."

Leo raised his eyebrows. "You know they've got a chemistry lab on the third floor. You could probably check that mango for sentience."

"Unnecessary." Rucha waved a hand at him dismissively. "It already whispered my name when I opened the box."

Hawthorne watched them volley surreal banter like it was a survival tactic in itself. It kind of was, she realized.

Leo leaned against the prep counter, setting the notepad down gently next to the scallion ramekins. “Honestly, if the mangos are only mildly haunted, they’re ahead of most of our seed bank inventory. Anything else threatening to come alive in there?”

Rucha flipped her clipboard theatrically and scanned her notes. “The most egregious sins are a couple of unlabeled bags of what I think is powdered mustard, one suspicious barrel of flour that keeps shifting slightly when no one’s near it, and a spice tube labeled ‘meat essence,’ which I refuse to touch.” She paused. “Also, someone hoarded thirty-five packets of black pepper in a mints tin and labeled it ‘Emergency Kick.’”

Leo chuckled. “Okay, weirdly relieved you’re the one handling all of this.”

“You’re welcome,” Rucha said with a theatrical bow.

Hawthorne stirred the congee slowly, listening to the thick swirl of the rice as the heat settled into something close to perfect. It had reduced just enough for the egg ribbons to float gently on the surface. She tasted it again and nodded to herself. Just enough earthiness from the rice and heat from the chili packets to trick the tongue into comfort. They’d made it work.

It didn’t feel like disaster food; it just tasted like breakfast.

Outside, voices started rising, a low murmur of movement and curiosity drifting down the hall. Hawthorne glanced toward the doors and caught flickers of people beyond the narrow window. The scent must have traveled.

Leo picked up one of the smaller bowls and turned it over in his palms. “We doing plated service? Or… cafeteria mayhem?”

“Little of both,” Hawthorne said. “We’ve only got four ladles and one semi-functional scoop that screeches if it moves too fast. Everyone grabs a bowl and I’m ladling it out.”

Rucha added, “We’re also encouraging everyone to pretend they’ve already washed their hands.” She pinched her nose. “You know, until they *actually* wash their hands.”

"I think you've invented a genre," Leo said to Hawthorne with a gentle smile that made her stomach flip flop.

"Psychological food service?" she asked with a raised eyebrow.

"No. Cozy catastrophe cuisine."

Hawthorne laughed and the sound of it startled her. "I don't hate that."

Leo dipped his head, still playing with the empty bowl in his hands, then lowered it gently back to the counter. The moment dissolved slightly, the mood cooling into something quieter.

"People have been trying to call out all night," he said, voice lower now. "Still no internet connection, and long-distance lines are just... dead." He rubbed the back of his neck absently. "From what I gather, local numbers work sometimes, but it's patchy. A few students heard back from parents in town, people holed up in houses. Everyone's treating it like a severe storm emergency. Hunker down. Wait it out." He paused and looked up. "But the silence from anything outside our area? That's starting to sit weird with people."

Hawthorne felt it like a distant pressure in her chest, the weight of the unknown, slippery and constant. She moved the congee from the counter to its own large rolling cart, then began arranging the spoons alongside the topping ramekins. Her hands moved without needing direction. "You think the lines are just too overwhelmed?"

"I don't know," Leo admitted. "Could be. Could be something bigger." He gave a small, tired shrug. "That's what scares people. Not knowing if waiting it out means waiting a week for help, or longer." He emphasized the final word, suggesting that 'longer' might mean 'a very long time.'

Rucha leaned back with her arms crossed, lips pressed just barely into a line. "Nobody thinks they're the last people standing until the silence stretches long enough to make space for the thought," she said. "Then it settles in like a lazy cat and ruins the couch."

Hawthorne snickered at the imagery but then shook her head. "We're not the last people. Not even close. This isn't the end." She felt those words settle. Not with certainty, but with dogged, stubborn hope. It was really the only kind of hope she was familiar with, since her father died.

Leo looked at her with something halfway between admiration and fatigue. "Good. 'Cause I did not save three dozen packets of sugar just to go gently into the bland."

"You hoarded sugar?" Hawthorne narrowed her eyes.

He grinned. "I pretend it's for morale. It's really for bribes."

Rucha clapped her hands once. "Okay. I am officially declaring this a soft reopening of civilization. Kitchen's functional, food's hot, sarcastic flirting quota met."

"Oh, shut up," Hawthorne mumbled, ignoring the slight blush that bloomed adorably over Leo's cheeks and nose.

She pushed the cart out into the hallway toward the former lecture hall, where a loose line of sleep-creased survivors already waited with hopeful eyes. The hallway smelled faintly of industrial cleaner and anticipation. People straightened slightly when they saw her, some smiling, others blinking blearily through the general fug of morning-after trauma. There was no cheer exactly, but there was a sense of camaraderie and a quiet glimmer of gratitude no one quite knew how to voice yet. It definitely wasn't the full number of people, but it was still only seven a.m. So Hawthorne guessed a lot were sleeping in...probably the ones who managed to grab a couch in an office or something better than the floor. Her night on the floor, curled up next to her mother, was barely tolerable. She knew it was bad for her mother's rheumatoid arthritis, too, and vowed to find a better solution if they had to spend another night locked up inside the agri center.

Small victories, she thought, rolling the cart past a young man in board shorts and a sunhat, who saluted her with a butter knife as she passed. The doors to the lecture hall-turned-dining commons were propped open, and the makeshift tables were already half-filled. Fold-out chairs creaked, and someone had tucked an ancient CD player in the corner that played low instrumental jazz in a bid for ambiance, Hawthorne guessed.

Rucha called out behind her, "Breakfast is served! The porridge has arrived!"

Hawthorne chuckled under her breath, breathing in the scent of rice and scallion from her own rolling cart. She positioned the cart at the head of the space, near a chalk-dusted whiteboard where someone had written ZOMBIE MOVIE BISTRO in smeared block letters. With a long-handled ladle in one hand and the utensils laid out in washed wire baskets, she was ready.

"Alright," she called out, loud enough to rise over the jazz-stained hush. "Form a line. Bowl, spoon, and some patience, please!"

Muffled laughter twisted through the crowd as they lined up, some in slippers, some still wearing yesterday's jeans crusted with road grit and, in some cases that Hawthorne refused to think about, blood. The first person in line was Maggie. Sleep-mussed and still hugging a sticker-bedecked coffee tumbler, she blinked at Hawthorne in confusion.

"Porridge?"

"Technically, congee," Hawthorne said simply, ladling a scoop and sliding it into her waiting bowl with a practiced swirl.

"What...is congee?" she asked, examining the bowl curiously.

"Breakfast. Trust me, it's warm, and it loves you."

And it did.

For the next hour, Hawthorne served, one careful ladle at a time, smiling through fatigue and split-second judgments about portion balance. Older folks, she gave a little extra. She cracked a joke every tenth person or so, something about the "exclusive brunch menu" or how the chili oil packets counted as a full personality trait now. People didn't always laugh, some smiled with the shell-shock grin of new trauma, others just blinked blankly. But they lined up and they waited, and they ate her food.

If she could keep them feeling human for a little while, well, that was the point.

Somewhere near the end of the line, Maggie circled back with an empty bowl and a hopeful shrug. Hawthorne refilled it wordlessly and passed it back with a nod.

"No seconds for most," she said quietly. "But I heard you're on clean-up detail after breakfast. Fair's fair."

Maggie groaned like she'd just been handed a final exam. "Okay, but I'm fragile."

"You'll get extra coffee," Hawthorne promised, then pointed. "Dish bin, after." She tried not to think about how long the coffee would hold out.

Maggie sighed and shuffled off, clutching her second bowl like it might protect her from her assigned fate.

Carlos showed up not long after, still in the same hoodie from the day before, his sleeve pinned awkwardly.

"You survive the night?" Hawthorne asked.

"Define 'survive,'" he replied, picking up a bowl. "If you mean I didn't die and no rats tried to make a nest in my armpit, then yeah."

"Admirable goals," she muttered, handing him a generous scoop.

He took a whiff, grinned, then added, "You need post-breakfast help?"

"Maggie and Rucha are on dishes. You can join them, but no flirting or I'll make you clean out the grease traps solo."

Carlos gave a mock salute.

By the time the last bowl had been scraped empty, Hawthorne finally allowed herself to roll her shoulders and breathe like a person without an audience. Mendez, who had sat on the fringes and eaten quickly, had disappeared at some point to handle whatever organizational catastrophe Shelly had cheerfully identified as everyone's "five-alarm problem of the day." Hawthorne didn't envy her. She'd take dish duty and congee management over clipboard bureaucracy any day.

She walked slowly toward the corner where her mother had claimed a camp chair near the portable heater—the coveted "arthritis throne," as Maggie named it the night before. But as Hawthorne approached, that warm feeling began to melt into a knot.

Marla was sitting upright, smiling vaguely out the large windows that lined the eastern wall, but her hands were trembling faintly. Her knees were flexed tight, drawn in slightly, and her old green hoodie—threadbare from lovingly long use—was zipped all the way to her neck, as if layering against pain and cold both.

"You didn't take your meds," Hawthorne said quietly, crouching beside her.

Marla didn't look away from the windows. She sighed. "Sweetie, I'm saving them."

"For what, the apocalypse?" Hawthorne deadpanned. "Because I hate to be the one to break it to you, but we're in it right now. There's no special premiere night. No surprise boss level."

"I know, I know," Marla said, waving her hand weakly. "But there are only so many pills left. And if this lasts… if the pharmacies go…"

"If you're in this much pain during the second morning, what do you expect to be able to do by the fifth?" Hawthorne leaned closer, lowering her voice. "You can't help anyone if we have to carry you everywhere. We'll figure out meds later. Right now, I need you to be able to walk and think and talk without grimacing every three seconds."

Marla sniffed. "That's slander. I only grimace every four seconds."

"Please, Mama."

That one stopped her. The laugh she'd pretended to hold cracked, and her weathered hand reached slowly into her coat pocket. She pulled out the tiny orange bottle and glared at it like it had made personal insults about her herb garden.

Two white pills rattled like dice as she twisted off the lid. She swallowed them dry.

"There," she said. "Two ancient horse pills down the hatch. Can I go back to quietly judging your carrot chopping from across the room now?"

Hawthorne smiled, then leaned forward and hugged her tight. "You can always judge the way I chop carrots. It's tradition."

Then, as she pulled away, she added with a wink, "But only if you promise to teach Maggie how to use a peeler without causing a community incident."

Marla grinned through the wince she tried to hide. "Deal. But she's not allowed near turnips yet. That's expert level."

Hawthorne laughed, breathing it all in—the clatter of breakfast cleanup in the background, the scrape of chairs and soft chatter filling the once-silent lecture hall, and the scent of congee lingering like a gentle morning after a really weird dream. She grabbed the cart holding the now-empty congee pot and followed Carlos and Rucha, who were bickering over how to stack the empty bowls on the cart.

Maggie quickly took to cleaning up the prep stations and stove top while Carlos and Rucha continued to pretend they weren't flirting as they rinsed dishes and stacked them in the industrial dishwasher. Hawthorne made a mental note to check with Mendez about their water supply, because if clean water was an issue, they might have to ration how often to use the machine, if at all. Or electricity for that matter. She sighed as she pushed the carts out of the way.

Shelly skidded to a stop in the kitchen doorway like the brakes on her personality had finally failed. Her bun was half undone and she was wearing one of Maggie's hoodies, easily identifiable by the "Compost or Die" patch on the sleeve.

"Gate!" she wheezed, panting like she'd sprinted the length of a football field with sheer anxiety. "There are people—seven, I think—outside the fence. Mendez is headed down herself. They're being followed."

Rucha, mid-stacking, straightened like someone had just dinged a bell in her spine. "Followed?"

"Shufflers," Shelly confirmed, breath whooshing out between syllables. "Like six or seven of 'em. Not running, but close enough. Mendez and Eli are ready to keep the way clear."

Then she was off again, bolting down the hall.

"Shit," Hawthorne whispered.

"What does she expect us to do?" Rucha asked no one in particular. Carlos shook his head, but Hawthorne was already moving.

Outside, the morning clung to a strange hush. The sound of birds was absent, and the people Hawthorne saw were all standing in tense, small groups, not talking. The main walkway through the agri center had been swept clear recently of branches and debris and was now lined with chalk-painted arrows meant to guide foot traffic and, according to Shelly, maintain "a sense of calm trajectory," whatever that meant. It all blurred as she jogged past until she got to the open yard leading to the gate.

Dr. Mendez was already there, a sturdy silhouette with that ever-present shotgun balanced across her forearm like it was just another clipboard. Beside her stood Eli, stoic in his forestry jacket and practical boots, arms folded.

"Use your words!" Dr. Mendez called out.

Seven people cluster-huddled just outside the gate. They looked bedraggled, dirty, and terrified, but still moving and alert. One of them, a kid couldn't be more than fourteen, was frantically waving a dinner knife in the vague direction of the half-dozen shufflers trailing behind them.

The shufflers didn't charge.

They loitered. Stalked. Their movements weren't aggressive so much as... slow and strange. Deliberate. Like cows that had discovered bipedal movement and were deeply confused about it.

But Hawthorne was focused on one person. "Trudy!"

Hawthorne surged forward, half-jogging across the gravel path that curved around the raised beds of winter greens, her boots thudding against packed red clay still pocked from The Storm. Her stomach twisted in knots as she recognized the figure grasping the outer gate in both hands.

"Trudy!" she shouted again, louder this time, one arm already raised.

The woman started at her name, braids frizzed and damp with sweat, eyes wide behind her huge fashion sunglasses. She wore a ripped Mazzy Star t-shirt layered over a long-sleeved waffle top, splattered in something she definitely wasn't wearing for fashion's sake. Despite everything—smeared dirt on her cheeks, the terror behind every move she made—her mouth opened in a grin at the sound of Hawthorne's voice.

"*Hawk!!!!* Thank every god in the known universe," Trudy yelled back. "I was starting to think we'd missed the boat."

"You're not late," Hawthorne said as she came up beside Dr. Mendez without missing stride. "What the hell happened?"

"Zombies," Trudy clipped out, nodding hard toward the figures beyond the fence. "Kind of. They're not fast, but they're damned persistent. Creepy as shit. We've been dodging them for blocks."

Mendez didn't look away from the small herd approaching in the distance, her eyes scanning the group in a practiced sweep. Hawthorne followed her gaze and saw two older men, one limping and leaning heavily on a piece of PVC pipe, and three younger adults, all panting and haggard. Everyone but Trudy was wearing business casual. Trudy acted like she'd appointed herself their guardian angel, hovering between them and danger, even though she looked like she hadn't eaten or slept for a while.

"You know her?" Mendez asked Hawthorne sharply, nodding toward Trudy.

"Yeah. She's Daniel's sister," Hawthorne said, then realized that meant nothing to Mendez. "Yes, yes! I know her! Let her in, damn it!"

Mendez nodded once. "Open the gate. Eli, stay on my left."

Eli took three steps forward and stopped beside her, picking up an enormous woodsman ax that apparently had been sitting handle-up on the ground next to him. Leo jogged up from somewhere and stopped next to Hawthorne, his fierce eyes focused on the zombies closing in.

Several people slipped forward and yanked back the gate bolt, allowing Trudy and the others to run in. One shuffler moved faster than the others, roaring as he gained speed.

One of the people coming in nearly stumbled as she crossed the threshold, but she caught herself and immediately spun on her heel to face the approaching shuffler. Hawthorne thought she looked as if she should be hosting events at one of the sorority houses, but her voice shattered like dropped glass.

"*You can't catch me, you son of a bitch!*" she screamed, her entire body taut, vibrating with fury. "*You don't get to win this time!*"

Everyone froze, watching her pull a metal thermos from her designer purse and chuck it hard. Hawthorne revised her assumptions as, clearly, she had been a softball pitcher at some point. It clanged off the approaching zombie's shoulder with a dull, useless thunk. The thing barely flinched, its pace unchanged, sluggish but dogged. Up close, it looked less like a monster and more like a ruin of a person. Male, late twenties, maybe thirties. Dressed in a torn casual canvas jacket and cargo pants crusted with dirt and worse. Despite the slack face and clouded eyes, there was something genuinely unsettling in the way he reached forward, like he recognized her.

Mendez was already moving again, striding past the woman and leveling the shotgun, tilting it upward, angling for distance. She didn't shout a warning. She didn't hesitate.

She *waited.*

The shuffler crossed the painted perimeter line someone had spray-chalked on the outer walkway and lunged in that clumsy, off-human way. One arm jerked up. The sorority-softball-pitcher stepped back instinctively but otherwise didn't blink.

Mendez's shotgun barked once with one bright, instantaneous sound that cracked across the empty morning.

The zombie dropped like a hit puppet, knees folding, body slapping the gravel face-first.

No one, not even the woman, cheered.

For a long moment, there was just the sound of everyone breathing, shallow and loud. The air stank of cordite and shocked silence.

Eli slammed the gate shut and secured it, turning with a nod to Mendez, who nodded back.

Everyone turned toward the woman, who was still braced against the metal bars like she'd kept them closed herself by force of will alone. Her mouth trembled, but she tilted her head high like a battered cathedral still trying to be a landmark.

"She broke up with him yesterday, just before the storm hit," Trudy said quietly to Hawthorne. "Apparently, he's been chasing her ever since. Real piece of work, sounds like."

"No kidding." Hawthorne glanced from the woman to the body splayed motionless just beyond the gate. Unease slithered up her spine. She didn't know much about the woman, didn't even know her name yet, but she knew that kind of silence. Half trauma, half triumph.

Trudy blew out a breath, still leaning on the fence like it was a friend who wouldn't leave her. Her hand was bleeding, slashed across the knuckles with what had probably been a run-in with some pavement. Hawthorne stepped up beside her and gently hugged her. Trudy clutched at her, and they just stood there for a long moment while Mendez talked to the other survivors. Hawthorne felt Leo's hand on her shoulder, grounding her.

"Come on. We've got clean bandages, fresh food, and possibly the last working bathroom with actual toilet paper in a fifty-mile radius."

"I could use some food," Trudy muttered, letting herself be led.

As they moved back toward the Delacroix building, more people trickled out onto the paths or stood peeking from doorways, watching the slow-shuffling herd of zombies outside the fence stumble aimlessly past the perimeter. Most of them didn't seem interested in approaching, but it was impossible to tell if that was because they did not want to get shot or if they just didn't care to try and break in. They turned in disjointed slow circles or wandered off between the magnolia trees like they'd forgotten what they were doing.

Hawthorne couldn't stop watching them, even as she walked.

They weren't fast. They weren't ravenous, not like the horror movies had promised. But something about them was fundamentally wrong, like watching corrupted data limp around in yesterday's body. It tugged at the primal fear in her gut.

Leo walked beside the two women as they headed toward Jake's erstwhile "E.R." room.

"You notice?" he asked.

"What?" Hawthorne glanced at him, one hand on Trudy's elbow to keep her steady.

"The others. They didn't move like predators. They moved like sheep. He was the only one who seemed to be aggressive."

"Everything about them is weird," Hawthorne said with a shrug.

"They can be dangerous, like that guy after Mackinzie," Trudy offered. "That's one reason I decided to make a break for it. We were trapped at the office."

"Those your coworkers?" Leo asked. Trudy nodded.

Leo frowned. "Did you see other survivors?"

"A few. Less than I expected. Plenty of zombies or whatever they are...some people I knew." She shuddered. "I assumed most people are just hiding." She pulled out her phone and shook it at Hawthorne. "But...hey, Hawthorne. I'm glad you're here. It's Daniel."

"Daniel? Did he turn into one of those things?" Hawthorne came to a stop, horrified by the idea.

"No! No, it's the opposite. He and Wren—they're still out there."

Hawthorne stared at her. "At home or in the truck?" Like The Gourmet Grinder, The Wrap & Roll was a step-van food truck, large and lumbering, and safe enough in the short term, she thought.

Trudy nodded. "The truck. Last clear phone call I got, they were outside the city. He'd been hired to work a family reunion picnic out by Robber's Rock and was on his way back in when the storm hit. He was trying to avoid the gridlock and got pushed off the bypass. Truck is stuck, and he's closed it up tight, but he's too far out. Lots of abandoned cars and no cops or anyone, other than those things. I wanted to get to him, but I felt bringing the others to someplace safe first was the best plan." She glanced over her shoulder. "Especially when Mackinzie's ex started after us."

Trudy's words hit Hawthorne in waves, dissonant beneath the surface calm she'd fought so hard to keep together that morning.

Daniel. Out there. Alive.

He and his husband had fed her when she was between gigs. He'd shared his personal sourdough starters, let her steal pickled lemons in chipped mason jars, taught her how to improvise flavor from nothing but panic and dried herbs. He was stubborn, generous, and always half a second away from making the closest stranger try a sample. If he was with Wren, his six-year-old daughter, the sweetheart who once mistook turmeric for cheese dust and tried to flavor popcorn with it, then she couldn't just let them wait.

"He's still in the truck?" she asked, eyes scanning the horizon like Daniel might be driving into view any second now. "That thing's like locking yourself in a soda can after the end of the world."

"Right?" Trudy replied, urgency tightening her voice. "He said they have food, of course, and the truck's got batteries, and that solar pad thing Adrien installed, but they're still stuck on the incline, and the windows aren't reinforced. They're sitting ducks."

Hawthorne turned to Leo, her expression already somewhere halfway between plea and resolution. "We have to go."

Leo exhaled slowly, rubbing a thumb along the warn leather edge of his tool belt like it might offer him advice. "Yeah. I agree."

She blinked. "You... do?"

"You think I haven't heard half the student body and most of my colleagues moaning about the 'grilled balsamic portobello miracle man' all these years?" he said with a crooked smile. "The Wrap & Roll is practically an official Calloway-Hayden institution. Anyway, what good is surviving if we don't help other survivors?" He turned to Trudy. "We'll help."

He looked at Hawthorne and met her eyes, something heavier sat behind his easy tone. Weight honed from yesterday's disaster, she thought.

"But we do it smart," he continued. "We talk to Mendez *first*. We get supplies. Maps. A route. And we scope who's willing to come, because doing a rescue run half-cocked is asking to die heroic and pointless."

"I don't want to wait too long," Hawthorne said, jaw tensing. "He's good at rationing, but if something breaks... if something gets in—"

"Then we prep fast," Leo cut in, voice low but firm. "I trust your gut, Hawthorne. But I'm not letting you go out there alone."

Hawthorne gave a tight laugh, the kind that cracked the tension just enough to let the adrenaline move without splintering. "Fine. No solo hero nonsense," she agreed. "But if Mendez says no, I'm still going."

"We're not going to her for permission," Leo said, already shifting into planning mode. "We're going for backup."

Trudy glanced between the two of them, her eyes wide but hopeful. "That bad-ass butch with the illegal shotgun? I think she'll go for it."

Leo looked shocked for a second before laughing so hard he had to bend over to catch his breath.

"I don't think it's illegal. We're open carry in this state," Hawthorne said thoughtfully over his laughter.

"We're on a *university campus*, Hawk. It's one-thousand percent illegal." Trudy grimaced. "Not that I'm arguing with her about it."

"Wise."

They gave Leo a second to recover. "Yes, the well-regarded, PhD-holding professor Dr. Mendez." He shook his head.

"You think she'll actually sign off on this?" Hawthorne asked.

"If we make a plan that doesn't sound like a suicide pact," Leo replied, "I think she might give us a truck and a walkie-talkie."

"That's your measure of approval?" Hawthorne asked, smiling despite herself.

"It's the Mendez Standard," he said. "An open hand, a project map, and a work truck."

Hawthorne turned her face into the breeze, feeling the breeze pull at her sleeves, curling through the seams of her focus. She imagined Daniel inside the truck, Wren asleep on a bench next to a bucket of greens, the doors barred with a broom handle or something.

"We'll talk to her after we get Trudy seen too," she said finally, starting to walk again.

Trudy just nodded wearily, and Leo offered a short, solemn nod.

As they entered Delacroix alongside Trudy, the clink of dishes and rise of weak laughter down the hallway welcomed them back. Life had resumed here—messy, quiet, human—and it was worth protecting. But Hawthorne's mind was already charting roads on instinct: the back highways, the dormant traffic lights, the half-forgotten cut-throughs that might be clear of pile ups and abandoned cars. Her pulse tapped out a rhythm: rescue, return, repeat.

Mendez was pragmatic, but Hawthorne had to believe that, surely, she could make room for one rescue run among all the chaos.

CHAPTER 6
Rescue 101

Mendez closed the office door behind them with a soft but final snick, the kind that said whatever happened in this room would not be heard beyond it. She turned back toward the group. Her eyes scanned the four of them, brows tight with quiet calculation.

The office itself was the acme of high-level administrative academia, featuring wood-panel walls, a wide desk scattered with paperwork and hard-copy spiral bound manuals, and an old, black, overfilled filing cabinet sitting quietly in the corner. In one corner stood a long oval meeting table, worn executive chairs arranged like people might still gather weekly to debate the budget. Hawthorne had noticed the sign on the door identified Mendez as the director of the agri center, so it made sense. Hawthorne's father, who had been a literature professor for an agricultural university, had a much smaller office in comparison.

Shelly stood near the doorway with a clipboard in one hand and a marker tucked behind one ear. Eli leaned quietly against a tall bookshelf, arms crossed like a displeased feral cat—if a *big* cat, like a panther or something. Hawthorne decided to stay out of his way.

Mendez crossed behind her desk but didn't sit. She rested both hands on the edge, elbows locked, grounding herself in place with authority that demanded respect.

"Well," she said with crisp efficiency. "You asked for a private meeting. What's on fire?"

Trudy sucked in a quiet breath through her nose, then looked at Hawthorne, clearly implying "now or never."

"It's my friend," Hawthorne said. Her voice was even, but the worry she felt made her feel like she was squeaking. "Daniel Phạm, owner-operator of The Wrap & Roll."

Mendez's eyes lit up with recognition, as Hawthorne had hoped.

"He's out past the bypass, in his food truck with his daughter, Wren. He's trapped because the storm pushed the truck off the road."

Mendez didn't react at first. She just stared, hard and thoughtful. Hawthorne was starting to feel sorry for any undergrads who had to face that expression.

"Trudy got a message from him right before she made it here," Leo added, stepping up to her side. "They were trying to come back into the city when everything hit. The truck's intact, and they're barricaded inside and waiting for help. But the roads there are probably packed with cars and shufflers by now."

Trudy held up her phone like a talisman. "I've still got the last text, but cell signal's been going in and out since this morning."

"So," Mendez said with one raised eyebrow, "you want to stage a rescue."

Hawthorne nodded once. "Yeah."

Eli exhaled sharply and looked at Mendez with the expression of a man who'd just been told someone wanted to put a thousand-acre wildfire out by themselves. "You're talking about getting back on the roads," he said carefully. "Roads we haven't fully scouted. Cars stopped, visibility low. And if that little herd from earlier was anything to go by, there's no telling how many of them are wandering around out there."

Shelly made a low, nervous sound. "And the shufflers—we *are* calling them that, right? Zombie-adjacent, but not? Sorta? They're weird. Too slow sometimes, too fast others. We don't have a good behavioral model yet." She ended her statement with confidence.

"They're zombies. Of course they're weird," Hawthorne countered.

"That's not the only concern," Mendez cut in, sharp and firm. She circled her desk with slow, measured steps, approaching the meeting table thoughtfully. Hawthorne felt her back stiffen as Mendez paused there, one hand settling lightly against the top of a worn binder that looked to be stuffed full of old paper maps.

"I'm responsible for nearly two hundred people at this point," Mendez said. "This goes beyond my job description of director to being a leader responsible for the lives of the people seeking shelter here, which means balancing logistics: food, morale, structural integrity—literal and emotional. If I send out people on a non-essential mission, that compromises our resources. And our people. All of them."

Hawthorne met her gaze and stepped forward until she felt the chill of the meeting table through her shirt. "And what makes Daniel and his daughter non-essential?" She shook her head. "He needs help, and we can help him."

Mendez's mouth made a small, immovable line. For a long moment, she didn't speak. Then she straightened up and started talking as if to a class of freshmen. "We *can*, sure. But while Fairhope is one of the smaller cities in this state, that's still nearly one hundred thousand people. I saw a good number of them turn into zombies, but we're living proof that not everybody did. And Carlos is proof that getting swiped by one doesn't 'turn' you like the horror movies claim. That means there are a lot of people who might be in the same situation that your friend Dan is in." She shook her head. "I want to help people as much as you do, but it's a risk. Whose life do I put on the line to save them? Is it more responsible for people to stay in place, keep to safe shelter until the National Guard shows up?"

She asked the question and Hawthorne felt like she was being quizzed and barely resisted the impulse to raise her hand. "It is, I agree. But here's the thing: other people aren't asking for help. Dan, by way of his sister, is. Most people are probably trapped in buildings, at work or at home, where they are reasonably safe. Dan isn't." She took a deep breath. "His daughter Wren is like my own niece, and she's only six. Please." She stopped short of saying, "Let us go or I'm going anyway," but Mendez seemed to hear it anyway.

Leo stepped forward, tapping the binder of maps, his tone steady. "Hawthorne grew up here, and I've lived here for ten years. We know the area and can take back routes and side roads. From what we saw, road-blocking pile-ups are rare. It's mostly abandoned cars skewed to the side. We can get there, assess the situation, and extract him and the girl, if not salvage the truck."

Eli nodded from his spot by the bookcase, voice quiet but certain. "Three work trucks in the shed adjacent to the barn. All diesel, all topped off. One of them even has a winch."

Leo spread his hands, palms open like he was laying out a simple truth. "We take two trucks. Just me and Eli. We bring radios, backup fuel, supplies. We avoid contact where possible, and we don't go sightseeing."

Shelly's pen scribbled frantically on her clipboard as she murmured, "Two-person team, estimated fuel window... uh, two hours round-trip with margin? Hmmmm."

Hawthorne stood at the edge of the meeting table, staring at the dulled sheen of its faux woodgrain and thinking about cooking. About food. About getting to people who were waiting to be rescued.

Leo's plan was clean and logical. Two people, two trucks, in and out. Grab Daniel and Wren, the supplies in his food truck, nothing else. And if she'd been watching from a distance—if this wasn't Daniel, if this wasn't Wren, if the person stuck out there with an aging propane fridge and a box of soba noodles wasn't someone who once called her his "culinary sister from another mister"—she might've thought it was perfect.

But she wasn't watching from a distance.

This wasn't just logistics. It was a rescue operation, yes, but she realized with a flash of insight that it was also *opportunity*.

A *second* food truck. Another mobile kitchen. Another set of wheels that could be used to help more people.

Hawthorne let her fingers curl loosely along the edge of the meeting table, the familiar laminate drag grounding her as thoughts slotted into place one after the other, like trays in a prep line.

Leo's plan was safe, focused, efficient. The kind of plan that would get Daniel and Wren back with minimal risk. A kind of slow-breath approach to heroism that she admired, even envied a little.

But that wasn't the whole meal.

"Dirty clothes," she said, finally, her voice quieter than earlier but no less certain. She looked at Mendez directly, who looked back with a confused head tilt.

"Dirty clothes?"

Hawthorne plucked at her shirt. "We're all wearing yesterday's clothes. Does this place even have showers for us to use?"

"Yes, over in the barn," Shelly piped up.

"Okay, but soap? Shampoo? Laundry detergent? My mother has her emergency stash of medicines, but that only lasts for a week, and all the rest of her meds are at home. She can't be the only one who needs meds, and everyone here needs at least a few changes of clothes. We can't just hole up here and hope for the best. Don't you see?"

"Hawk, what's this got to do with Danny?" Trudy asked pointedly.

"It's got to do with the fact that General York Air Force Base is one hundred twenty miles away, but we have not seen a flyover since the storm hit. That there are no emergency broadcasts on the radio telling to stay in place or anything else. There are shockingly few survivors that we can tell, and many of them might be in dangerous situations. Trudy and her co-workers got here on luck alone. That right now we might be all we've got for who knows how long. Another day? Week? Month?"

"It took nearly three weeks for the National Guard and FEMA to get to Limping Duck Hollow after the flood of '09," Eli offered, and they all nodded, remembering that multi-layered tragedy.

Hawthorne decided to strike while the burner was hot. "We keep thinking in terms of short-term survival, but Daniel doesn't have the luxury and, honestly, we need his truck."

Mendez's eyebrows rose. "His truck?"

"Yes! That food truck is more than just Daniel and Wren's bunker on wheels." She paused, heartbeat steadying against the panic she hadn't fully registered until now, realizing that they were looking to her for answers. The college dropout, the food truck chef. What business did she have telling them what to do? But she *knew* she was right.

"It's a mobile kitchen, Mendez. A fully functional, self-powered commercial kitchen."

From across the room, Shelly blinked, clearly flicking some invisible mental sticky note into a new column. Leo looked up, frowning with what could either be interest or impending skepticism.

"So?" Mendez asked evenly. "I don't mean that dismissively. We're not the National Guard. Hell, we're not even FEMA. We've already got nearly two hundred people here, and at best, we can probably support twice that for a few months, what with the gardens, greenhouses, and stored supplies. But that's it. Search and rescue is all well and good, but we can't feed even a tenth of the city population indefinitely." Mendez spoke with grim authority.

Leo nodded slowly, as if against his will.

"*That's my point!*" Hawthorne insisted. "We have no idea when the National Guard will get here, much less how much they can bring in to help us. But food is out there! We're not centrally located, true. Out in the county proper are dozens of working farms. We've got two big-box grocery stores and dozens of dollar stores, with supplies just sitting around. Right now, it's isolated survivors who could end up starving while we let scattered resources and food rot on the shelves."

"Wait." Mendez held up a hand to stop her. "Are you saying we should be the local command center for this crisis?"

Everyone looked at each other for a moment.

Hawthorne blinked, more startled by the sudden accuracy of the question than by its weight. But it fit perfectly, a puzzle piece she hadn't known was in her hand until it clicked neatly into place.

"Yeah," she said. "I mean... *yeah*. Why not? We've got facilities trucks for doing supply runs, and with two food trucks as mobile relief stations, we can assess who is still alive and what help people need."

Around the room, no one moved. Even the scuff of Shelly's pen on the clipboard ceased.

Hawthorne decided to keep going.

"We're already halfway there," she continued. "You've got supplies, structure, strong leadership. You've got people looking to you for stability, and you've got a place that can grow food, repair gear, create shelter. That means this isn't just our safe spot anymore. This could be the anchor for getting through this and even rebuilding when the lights come back on."

"The lights are on." Shelly pointed at the ceiling then cringed. "Oh, you meant metaphorically. Right."

Leo straightened slowly beside her, his face unreadable, but his stance shifting like a man realizing he'd been standing too small for the space he was actually in.

Mendez didn't smile. But she tilted her head slightly, like she'd just heard something she hadn't been quite expecting but was glad to hear.

"So you're pitching us as..." she paused, "the FEMA of the apocalypse?"

"FEMA takes time to gear up. Time we don't have," Hawthorne said. "I'm pitching us as the food truck that finds you first."

That landed and even Eli made a quiet sound that might've been amusement. Shelly mouthed the words "bumper sticker" at her clipboard.

"I'm serious," Hawthorne said, warming to it now. "We get Daniel's truck out, we double our capacity to be mobile. It's not about feeding people once, they'll need it again tomorrow, and the day after, and maybe even next week. We could get organized and stage recovery. Find more trucks. More survivors. Set up routes. Set up neighborhood kitchens. That's how things kept running in Katrina and Florence and all the others, at least at the edges—unofficial mobile support units, unofficial rescue teams. People showing up to help when the institutions couldn't."

Leo looked over at her, then something dawned behind his eyes, catching light. "She's right," he said, slowly. "If the real support's bottlenecked somewhere else, then we start local." He shot Hawthorne a wry grin. "And everyone does need a change of clothes, much less their meds or whatever else. Many folk here got family at home. No tragedies so far, but communications are already unreliable locally, and down at the national level. The networks are only as good as their weakest link."

Hawthorne felt her head bobbing up and down. "Yeah! This is just a trial run, going out to save Daniel and his daughter and get the lay of the land."

Mendez exhaled through her nose, paced once around the desk, then stopped. She tapped the top of her desk once, twice, letting the rhythm settle the air in the room. Then she looked up, her gaze sharp and directed right at Hawthorne.

"Fine," she said. "Provisional approval, based on what you find when you get out there. If it's clean, quick, and Daniel's truck is intact, we bring it in. But if it's a disaster site?"

Leo's face tightened just a notch. He knew where this was going and Hawthorne suspected she did, too.

"You don't linger," Mendez finished. "You don't risk it to prove a point. No hero moves, no second tries. This isn't a crusade, it's a scouting and recovery mission. You all are going out there to see how things stand; are people leaving? Are hordes of zombies shuffling around waiting for dinner to drive by? We need to know what we're up against before we start up emergency services. Understood?"

Leo and Eli both nodded.

Then she turned squarely to Hawthorne. "And you're going with them."

It hit like a dropped pan. For a full second, Hawthorne just blinked at her.

"I—what?"

"Your idea. You started this," Mendez said, tone softening just a hair. "You made the case. That means you carry some of the weight. Plus, if this whole food-truck-outreach idea's going to work, we need someone who actually knows the logistics—what's viable, what's not. That's not Eli. And it sure as hell isn't me."

"Or me," Leo said laconically.

Hawthorne's mouth opened, then closed. It wasn't fear exactly, though the thought of crawling back through storm-raked roads to face whatever waited near the bypass left her stomach twisting slowly. It was more surprise. She hadn't expected to be part of the retrieval. She'd imagined pacing back and forth on campus until they returned. Maybe getting Rucha to help draw up contingency meal plans or turning the kitchen supply lists into updated inventory charts.

But from the expectant look Mendez was giving her, there wasn't room for backing out, only moving forward.

"I understand," she said, rolling her shoulders back. She had worked the college bar scene during St. Patrick's Day every year since she was seventeen. She could do this.

Leo was wearing a slight frown, but Hawthorne ignored him for the moment, figuring they could talk later.

"Good." Mendez finally moved to sit behind her desk, the chair creaking faintly beneath her. "Skies are clear, so you leave at ten a.m., which gives you an hour to get ready. Shelly, help with prepping supplies. Fuel, first aid, comms, ration packs."

Hawthorne thought that was a bit of overkill for a quick run out to the bypass on the north side of town. But then, they were in the middle of a zombie apocalypse. What did she know?

Leo gave a tight nod and turned for the door almost immediately, exchanging a wordless glance with Eli, who peeled himself off the bookcase and followed. Shelly hesitated long enough to pull two highlighters from her pocket before ducking after them, muttering something about fuel cell readings and bandage sizes.

That left Hawthorne standing in the still-quiet room, the descriptor "The Food Truck That Finds You First" still echoing faintly behind her ribs like a bell that had only half-faded. Mendez raised an eyebrow in a silent "Anything else?" question, but Hawthorne shook her head to clear her thoughts before skeedaddling out the door.

Outside the office, she passed a few people, their heads down, purposeful. The agri center hadn't quite become a refugee camp. Not yet. But it was already bearing the weight of its new role. It was obviously starting to sink in with people that help was not going to be immediately forthcoming, which made Hawthorne switch directions from the kitchen to go find her mother.

After a few false leads, Hawthorne found Marla in one of the smaller greenhouses, which seemed to be devoted to seedlings, talking to some kind of plant. Tomatoes? Hawthorne wasn't sure what any of the rows of seedlings were. She only dealt with *ingredients*, not farming.

"Hey," Hawthorne said, voice low.

Marla turned, her posture loosening just a bit when she saw who it was. But one look at Hawthorne's face obviously chased her ease away.

"What happened?" she asked, already straightening, wiping her hands on the hem of her coat.

Hawthorne stepped closer, lowering her voice. "It's Daniel. Trudy got a message from him this morning before she got here. He and Wren were out to the country with the truck on a family reunion job. He was trying to loop back into town before the storm hit, but they got forced off the road and stuck. They're barricaded inside the truck, just outside the bypass."

"Oh, God," Marla said, just enough air behind the words to register. "And they're still out there?" Her face paled slightly, one hand settling on the edge of the greenhouse table, fingertips brushing a pot labeled 'Early Girl.' "He's waiting for help that isn't coming."

Marla's eyes flicked beyond her shoulder, as if looking for something outside the greenhouse. Then she pulled herself back with a deep inhale. "What's the plan?"

"We're going after them—me, Leo, and Eli." Hawthorne said it plainly, like she had rehearsed it in her head to feel more real. "Two trucks with diesel and radios. It's a scouting trip, mostly. If Daniel and Wren are okay, we bring them back; if The Wrap & Roll can be salvaged, we'll bring that back too."

Her mother stared at her for a long beat. Hawthorne recognized: not angry, not panicked. But careful.

"You're going?" Marla asked, voice measured but not enough to hide her worry.

"I am," Hawthorne said. "I pushed for the rescue mission, and Mendez greenlit it contingent on me being part of it."

Marla turned back to the greenhouse table, fussing absently with a mesh cover over one of the seedling trays, though her mind was clearly several miles away.

"You know I love Daniel," she said softly. "He and Adrien and Wren are family, and I want them back, with all my heart."

Hawthorne waited. The tone said there was a "but" rolling in.

"But," Marla continued, looking up with eyes that suddenly made Hawthorne feel very much like a kid again, "I also love you. And everything in me says I should be keeping you here."

"I know." Hawthorne leaned forward, tilting her forehead until it rested lightly against her mother's. "But I have to do it, Mom," she said before pulling back.

Marla's eyes softened the way they always did when Hawthorne leaned into something with her whole heart. She told Hawthorne once that she reminded her of Hawthorne's father.

"It's not just about Daniel," Hawthorne admitted, voice low. "I mean, yes, obviously. But this could be something more important than just a couple of survivors! If we get his truck back, it's not just two more mouths to feed. It's a moving kitchen, a supply point. We could take food out to people who can't go far in the city with those monsters around. Not everyone's going to be able to find *this* place, and the city's not small. Most people are probably still holed up in their homes, scared and hungry. And if they're not lucky enough to be with someone smart like you, or if they're injured..."

"And if they aren't themselves anymore?" Marla said gently, no malice in it, just quiet recognition. "We don't know how many made it through... that first night."

Hawthorne swallowed hard. Her fingers found the edge of the greenhouse table and pressed into it. "I know," she whispered. "But *some* did. We've got two hundred in the agri center already. There could be thousands more, just waiting for help, like Daniel. We can't just feed ourselves over and over and wait for someone else to fix it. If the system's broken, and I think it is, it's up to us to start building the next one."

Marla watched her. Then, she smiled—slow and deep, the kind that moved in layers. Sadness. Fear. But under it all, pride. "You always liked to be bossy," she said. "You'd be six years old in the yard directing potluck logistics like Eisenhower." She reached out and fixed a strand of Hawthorne's hair behind her ear. "But this is bigger than the kitchen at Roger's Diner."

"I know," Hawthorne said with a grimace. Roger's Diner was a large chain that served large burgers on large platters. It was the biggest kitchen she had run, a major step up in her career she thought at the time. But the franchise owner was an idiot, and the place had shut down, leading to her working for Frank out of desperation. Fairhope just wasn't big enough for too many large restaurants, especially when the students weren't in town. "But it still starts with food, Mom. It always has."

Marla nodded, exhaling slowly and they hugged briefly, transferring something wordless and vital.

Hawthorne stood up and stepped back with a breath that felt steadier than the air had been a moment ago. "I'll bring them back," she promised.

"As long you bring *you* back too." Her mother's smile was a little watery, but still strong and supportive as always.

Hawthorne left her to the seedlings and went to look for the facilities building to join up with Leo and Eli. After stopping three people and getting three different instructions on how to get there, she discovered that the facilities building was only a quarter-mile from where she had started. Still, the walk felt longer than it should have. Hawthorne's legs were restless with anticipation, but her brain was doing its best to climb back up the wall of everything she'd just said. Had she really pitched herself as Zombie FEMA's head chef? Storms and shufflers and food trucks as lifelines?

It all sounded a little absurd when replayed in her own head. But then, she'd never done anything small, not when it mattered. She had dropped out of college to help take care of her father as he died and would never regret that choice. This, she figured, was not much different.

It was a different form of apocalypse was all.

She cut through the open commons, passing a few people working in a garden plot, some of them clearly not knowing what they were supposed to do but trying to follow the directions being given. One of them who looked young enough to be an undergrad tossed Hawthorne an uncertain nod as she passed. No one quite knew what role they were playing yet in this new version of Fairhope.

The facilities building was smaller than she expected, but the garage attached to it was a massive white-washed concrete garage with peeling paint with one side overtaken by a winding honeysuckle vine. She could hear the clatter and low hum of prep work even before stepping inside.

The big space smelled like diesel and tool oil, like something productive and industrial. One of the trucks had its hood up, and beneath it, Eli was poking at something with the concentration of a man who only had one backup plan and was currently holding it together with elbow grease and prayer. Leo stood nearby, sorting through a pile of hard-sided cases, some stacked with radio gear, some with medical supplies, and others that looked suspiciously like scavenged canned goods refashioned into emergency rations.

"There she is," Leo said as she approached, his voice casual but warm. “We were starting to think Mendez pulled you for a follow-up TED Talk.”

“Just had to talk to my mom,” Hawthorne said, moving to help without being told. Leo nodded in understanding and just pointed to a few packs on the ground which looked like medical supplies. She started loading the packs into the cab of the second truck. “She’s on board, mostly.”

“Mostly doesn’t get you out of the mission,” Eli muttered, yanking a wrench from the toolbox and muttering something about clogged fuel lines. “You good with all this?”

“Yeah,” she said, automatically, and then, more firmly, “I mean, yes. I’m here now.”

Leo glanced her way, his eyes catching the slight hesitation. He motioned with his head toward the side of the garage, somewhere a little quieter, out of the immediate clang and hum of Eli’s mechanical muttering. Hawthorne hesitated mid-pack-stuffing, then followed, brushing her palms off on her jeans as she rounded the corner.

The light was softer here, filtered through the high grimy windows. The buzz of fluorescent bulbs and metal tools dulled to a low background hum. Leo leaned against the wall, arms crossed like he was trying to keep his own nerves from spilling out his sleeves. He glanced at her, then away, then back again. “Look,” he started. “I know you’re not new to pressure.”

Hawthorne tilted her head. “But?”

“But this is different.” He exhaled, scrubbing a hand across the back of his neck. “Storms. People turning into... whatever the hell. And now you’re heading out into it. When I pitched going light and fast, I figured leaving you back at base would be the part that kept it simple and safe—for you.”

That did something strange to her heart, a slow twist like someone was adjusting the flame level without warning. “Simple and safe wasn’t an option once I opened my mouth in that meeting,” she said, trying to go for light but ending up only half-laughing.

Leo smiled faintly. “I know. You had a point. Hell, you may have mapped out the only plan we’ve got with legs. I just—” He looked away, like he was trying to wrestle the words into a shape that wouldn’t betray how deeply he actually gave a damn. "I just don't want something to happen to you because of it."

It wasn't the kind of thing she expected, not from him. Not from quiet, sharp Leo, who usually spoke in half-smirks and laconic shrugs, someone she had only seen once or twice a week on the other side of the pickup window. It caught her off-guard.

"I'm not looking for a hero badge," she said, a little softer. "I just... I had something to offer, and I offered it. You know?"

He nodded, but his brow furrowed like that answer didn't make it entirely out of the worry woods.

"We've got a plan," she added. "I trust us. And I trust you."

That earned a more genuine smile, small but warm. "Okay," Leo said, rolling one shoulder like he was trying to shake off some of the tension. "You trust me, I trust you. I'll take it."

Hawthorne laughed quietly, surprised at how much lighter she felt in that moment. "Tell you what," she said, leaning a shoulder against the wall beside him. "When we get back, I'll make you a real meal. Good old hot comfort food. Something that doesn't come out of a can."

He raised an eyebrow, the corner of his mouth lifting. "Is this how you bribe people into surviving an apocalypse? Promising casseroles?"

"Not casseroles," she said, mock-offended. "Honest-to-God bánh mì. I've got three cans of pickled daikon already hidden in the back pantry, and Rucha found a stash of not-stale baguettes in the freezer."

Leo's eyes lit up at that. "You're dangerous, Hawthorne."

She gave him her best innocent look. "Compliments get you extra cilantro."

They stood in comfortable silence for a moment, the kind that didn't need to be filled. Outside, the sounds of final prep drifted in with Eli tapping something or another and the mechanical whir of a radio being tested, and Shelly's voice rising in protest about "Tape colors meaning things!"

When Hawthorne glanced at Leo again, his gaze was on her, steady and open in a way it hadn't been before. "I meant it," he said quietly. "Be smart out there. Not just brave."

Her chest tightened again. That same surprising twist was not quite fear, not quiet nerves, but the unfamiliar weight of being seen and cared for, right when it counted.

"I will be," she said. "And you too."

They lingered in that moment until Eli yelled, "Time to move out, people!"

Leo grinned like a tether snapping loose.

"Back to work," he said, pushing off the wall.

"Back to work," she echoed, falling into step beside him.

Whatever came next, including storm-wracked roads or zombies with twitching hands and blank eyes, their wheels were about to hit the asphalt. Hawthorne was scared but confident, knowing that this trip was more than just a rescue mission for Daniel and Wren.

CHAPTER 7
End Times Country Buffet

The truck bumped hard over a clogged drain at the edge of Eugenia Lane as Leo drove around an abandoned car, rattling everything in the cab and jostling Hawthorne's knee against the glove compartment. Outside, Fairhope passed by in eerily quiet snapshots: curbside mailboxes tilted from wind damage, flyers pressed to windows like they were trying to warn someone in silence, and a grocery cart tangled in the remnants of a magnolia tree halfway across someone's lawn.

Even having lived through the storm, Hawthorne was shocked to see just how violent it was. While buildings were still standing, there were plenty of tree branches impaled through windows or smashed on top of cars.

They'd been on the road for maybe twenty minutes, shadowing Eli's truck two car lengths ahead, and so far, nothing had tried to eat them.

Which was both reassuring... and not.

"This is weirder than I expected," she said quietly, her hand curled loosely around the door handle.

Leo didn't take his eyes off the road, but his fingers tightened slightly on the wheel. "Yeah. Too quiet?"

"That, but also, *where is everyone?*"

She stared out the window, past the crumpled remnants of her hometown. There was stripping on banners downtown where Fairhope's annual "Jump into Spring" festival had been advertised just three days ago. Posters for plays and community yoga that survived now hung limp, soaked through from the storm and sagging against business windows. It could have been the regular aftermath of any severe storm, except the sidewalks were *empty*. Cars sat abandoned, some crashed into each other, but not nearly as many as she'd imagined when they talked about "citywide collapse." It wasn't an apocalypse built of crumbling towers or scorched rubble.

It was just... quiet.

It was as if the majority of Fairhope had vanished sideways.

Here and there, shufflers loitered, but they weren't swarming like the movies had promised. Most of them drifted near parked cars or stood stalled in front of storefronts like they were waiting to be let in, arms slack, heads cocked. A few turned as the truck passed, but none gave chase. One older man in bloody jogging clothes blinked slowly, scuffing his foot along the yellow dividing line in the road like it was his only remaining purpose.

"They're not trying to stop us," Hawthorne said.

Leo grunted in agreement. "They're also not wandering in groups or heading somewhere specific. Not predator behavior and not herd behavior. I never thought I'd say this about *zombies,* but they are not behaving like any animal I know of. It's incredibly unnatural."

Unnatural was the word of the day, she decided.

She gestured absently at the notebook sitting propped up on her knees. Leo had asked her to try to keep a tally of all the zombies (shufflers?) she saw, but neither of them had expected it to be so easy or exact. Every block or so she jotted down small numbers, and while they were adding up, it still wasn't anywhere near a zombie horde.

The sunlight caught on a broken window up ahead, flaring gold through the grime as they passed the shell of a corner pharmacy. A shuffler stood just outside the shattered entrance, its head moving slightly in their direction, but it didn't follow. Just tilted, like maybe it had heard something interesting.

Hawthorne adjusted the seatbelt strap where it chafed along her collarbone, notebook balanced on one thigh. Ninety minutes ago, she'd been ladling out congee and cracking jokes about chili packets saving civilization. Now she was keeping tallies of the undead, nervously watching for signs of ambush that never came. *Unnatural.*

She was about to note another lone shuffler parked beside a busted newspaper stand when something flickered in her peripheral vision. Her breath caught.

A figure.

She could tell right away that it was not a zombie, but something was off.

A woman in her thirties, wearing athletic leggings and an oversized hoodie, tangled ponytail swinging as if she'd been running. She looked glittery, like sunlight reflecting off of raindrops but also insubstantial. Hawthorne realized that she could see *through* the woman a little, as if she was made of fog.

She was standing in the middle of the sidewalk as they passed. Not staggering. Not charging. Just watching them as they passed. Her eyes met Hawthorne's, and they were full of grief and sadness.

...and then she was gone.

She had vanished. Just simply, utterly disappeared in an instant.

Her mouth opened, throat dry, Hawthorne sat silent a second too long.

"You okay?" Leo asked, glancing her way quickly before focusing on the road again.

"I..." She frowned back at the empty sidewalk, then shook her head. "I'm not sure."

His grip shifted subtly on the wheel again. "Talk to me."

"I just saw a woman," Hawthorne said slowly. "Back there. She was standing on the sidewalk and looked right at us."

"Alive?" Leo asked immediately, alert now. "I didn't see anyone." He glanced at the side mirror.

She hesitated. "I don't know. It looked like she was... glowing. Not in a radiation kind of way! Just—I don't know. Bright. Like her outline didn't belong in the scene. I swear I saw though her, you know, like a ghost?"

There was a beat of silence.

Leo exhaled through his nose like he was trying to dial back whatever part of his brain had briefly screamed *ghost?!?!?*.

"Could've been reflection," he suggested carefully. "Glass, wet pavement, weird light refraction."

"I know what I saw," she replied, but the certainty in her voice came with more doubt than confidence.

Leo's fingers tapped the steering wheel once, twice. He didn't scoff or try to change the subject, which she appreciated, but on the other hand, he didn't say much at all.

"Could've been someone in shock," he offered after a long pause. "What if she's just out of it?"

"Maybe," Hawthorne murmured. But no, she knew that wasn't it. There had been something about how the woman's eyes had tracked them—focused, intentional, and knowing instead of empty or dazed. She had been fully alert and then gone, like a light switched off when you're mid-blink.

She hunched closer to the passenger side door and peered at the side mirror, but all it showed now was the tail end of the pharmacy sign and a bank drive-thru sign.

"She looked real," she said, keeping her voice low. "Not like flesh and blood real, more like... emotionally real. Like she was a real person."

Leo, to his credit, winced only slightly. "'Emotionally real' sounds like something a poet says right before they vanish in the woods."

"Great. So I'm either hallucinating or already cursed," she said with a grim chuckle.

"We're all cursed, Hawthorne," he said dryly, eyes back on the road. "That's what *apocalypse* means."

That earned a small huff of a laugh from her. "Can I still claim it was a ghost if I wasn't scared of it?"

"I think that makes it worse. At least your average horror movie ghost does a jump-scare first." He glanced her way with a smile, which helped her mood lift a little.

She let her head rest lightly against the window. The chilled glass helped push back the sudden thrum behind her eyes. She wanted to believe it had been a trick of the sun, a weird smear on her glasses from leftover congee starch or rice vapors. But she wasn't lying, and she wasn't cursed. She had seen something like a ghost, *and it had seen her too.*

"Forget it," she mumbled. "Maybe I'm overtired. Or just fried from the adrenaline rush."

The silence returned, more thoughtful than tense now. The hum of the engine echoed between them, steady like a heartbeat. A row of box elders cut ragged shadows across the slope as they turned the last corner onto Mayfield Spur, the brush-thinned frontage road that paced the interstate and was known not-so-fondly as "the Spur."

Hawthorne caught her breath as they crept along the Spur, eyes flitting over the chaos left behind. The storm had been brutal here, with fewer buildings to break up gusts of wind and rain.

Cars lay scattered like a child had thrown a tantrum with their matchbox collection, with some nosed into ditches at odd angles, others still idling in the middle of the cracked pavement, front ends crumpled, airbags ballooned through broken windshields. One white sedan had been shoved clean onto the curb and was now half-submerged in a shallow drainage ditch, its hazard lights still blinking, a dying signal on loop.

There were no bodies.

No movement.

Just the eerie impression that everyone had been plucked away mid-action. Fast food wrappers clung to the fences, fluttering like prayers. A baby stroller sat overturned in the grass, empty but pointed toward the road like someone had been rushing away. A truck's back gate was swung wide open, the remnants of bottled water and granola bars scattered across the shoulder.

But no people. No ghosts and weirder still, no zombies. Had they been pulled somewhere else? How many people became zombies anyway?

It lodged a strange, unsettled feeling in Hawthorne's chest, a form of anxious fear that felt like static.

"Where did they all go?" she whispered.

Leo didn't answer, looking out the window with the same confusion she felt. "I at least expected bodies," he said apologetically.

They rolled past a large travel bus laid sideways across both lanes, its windows blown out and seats visible through the ripped frame. Hawthorne could see some blood spots on a few seats as they drove by, but otherwise it was just *empty*. Everything felt suspended in time.

As they cleared the curve, she spotted a child's backpack tangled in a barbed-wire fence with a bright pink unicorn on black canvas, soaked and slumped like it had given up. Beneath it, the mud still held the imprint of small shoes.

She turned away, pressing her nail into a corner crease of the notebook, feeling the paper give to pressure. She wrote furiously on it: "Children! Schools? Hospitals! Nursing homes?" She had no idea what to put after that, but figured that was Mendez's job, not hers anyway.

Eli's truck finally slowed almost to a crawl ahead of them, as they were close to the location Trudy had told them about. Past the curve, The Wrap & Roll truck came into view, tilted awkwardly down a grassy embankment halfway between the interstate and the Spur, the rear wheels half-sunk into the wet slope. Fortunately, Hawthorne did not see smoke or shattered windows. It was simply stalled, like someone had parked in a hurry and gravity hadn't played by the rules.

"Stop!" Hawthorne said sharply, already unbuckling.

Leo slowed to pull up behind Eli.

She was opening the door before the wheels rolled to a stop. Her boots hit the gravel with a scrape, and she was moving, jogging toward the truck before her head had settled from the impact of fresh air.

"Daniel!" she shouted, voice lifted with urgency. "Wren?"

No response from inside.

Leo caught up to her at the rear of the truck, a big machete in hand that had previously only ever been used to cut sod. Eli jogged up a second later with a rifle pointed at the ground, but his eyes doing a quick sweep of the surrounding embankment and the rise toward the tree line beyond.

"No movement," Eli muttered.

Hawthorne didn't bother with pleasantries. She was already at the driver's side door, scanning for signs of forced entry or blood. She let out a deep breath when she saw there wasn't any. The cab was locked, the windows intact but fogged a little from within, as if the last body heat had evaporated just hours ago.

She ducked to check under the truck. Nothing.

Nothing but wet grass and dirt and the slow dripping of leftover rainwater from the undercarriage.

Coming back around, she rapped twice on the passenger side with her knuckles. "Daniel! Wren! Come on, it's me—Hawthorne! You in there?"

No response.

The silence clawed under her rib cage.

She glanced at the electric keypad lock on the door, one of Daniel's retrofits.

"If they're passed out or hurt or trapped, they might not be able to answer," she said, already stepping toward the keypad. "I know the code."

Leo and Eli nodded, moving into a flanked stance on either side, not aggressive, just ready. They didn't need to say that they were expecting horrors and, for the moment, Hawthorne refused to believe it. She hesitated only a second before tapping in the six-digit code.

The keypad clicked green.

She pulled the handle.

The heavy door gave with a soft hiss of pressure release, swinging outward on its hinges. The inside smelled faintly of thawing vegetables and ginger. Cold air spilled out, but no sound, no rustling, no groans.

Food bins were stacked in their usual way with sauce bottles latched down for transit. The motion-activated overhead bulbs flicked dimly on, catching on the stainless steel countertops and stored prep bags. A clipboard hung by the sink.

But no people.

No Daniel.

No Wren.

Hawthorne stepped in fully, heart knocking somewhere beneath her ribs.

They weren't inside.

She turned back out, face drawn, voice tight. "They're not here." It was stating the obvious, but she had to say it to believe it.

Hawthorne's heart was doing laps somewhere in her throat as she turned in a slow, deliberate circle inside the truck's prep space, eyes darting over every familiar stainless steel surface, fingers twitching toward drawers and bins, the walk-in fridge door. Nothing out of place except the two people who should've been there, waiting for rescue.

Leo hovered just behind her, not saying anything, but he was at least a comforting presence.

She moved back toward the cab, shoes squeaking faintly against the thick rubber floor mats. Climbing up into the driver's seat felt surreal, like wearing someone else's coat and finding a ghost of their warmth still in the sleeves.

Daniel had always kept his truck clean. The cab still had that weird lemon-pine cleaner smell mixed with fryer oil and smoked paprika. There were crumpled receipts in the cup holder, a baby blue hoodie of Wren's shoved halfway under the jump seat. No sign of violence, Hawthorne thought gratefully as her eyes caught on a folded sheet of printer paper, taped dead center to the dashboard on top of the speedometer with two strips of blue masking tape.

Leo stepped closer, his knee bumping the driver's seat as he leaned in.

Hawthorne pried the note loose and opened it. Daniel's handwriting was quick-slanting and near-illegible, but she could read it anyway. She'd read dozens of his panicky dinner rush lists written just like this.

IF ANYONE FINDS THIS: TRIED TO HIDE OUT BUT ZOMBIES KEEP COMING. THEY BACKED OFF AT DAWN SO I'M TAKING MY SIX-YEAR-OLD DAUGHTER AND RUNNING FOR MORE SECURE LOCATION. TRYING FOR POLICE HQ, HEADED DOWN MCLEARY. MY SISTER WENT TO THE AGRI CENTER. IF YOU READ THIS, PLEASE LOOK FOR US. JUST ME AND MY LITTLE GIRL.

It was signed with his name and "8:45 AM" which was, she assumed, when he wrote the note and took off. She looked up out of the window, where not a single zombie was in sight. Had they *followed* Daniel and Wren? Her heart skipped a beat.

Hawthorne was already out the cab door headed to one of the trucks before Leo caught her by the elbow.

"We've got to go after them," she said, turning sharply. The note fluttered a little in her hand, crushed already from the grip she hadn't noticed tightening. "He has Wren. He was scared enough to abandon the truck, that wouldn't happen unless something was breathing down his neck!"

Leo didn't let go. "I get it. I do. But we shouldn't just leave the truck."

"She's six! They are in danger!" She yanked her arm out of his grasp.

"I understand!" he yelled back.

"Hey! Stop shouting!" Eli hissed at both of them as he walked up, looking tense. "We don't know what brings the shufflers out."

Hawthorne took a deep breath before starting again at a lower volume. "I'm not saying leave it forever. Just go rescue them *first*."

Leo shook his head. "You said it yourself: we're going to need trucks like this to help survivors. If we chase after him now, there is no guarantee we can come back for it anytime soon."

Hawthorne clenched her jaw, staring hard at him like maybe that would force another answer out.

"We're not abandoning them," he went on carefully. "We're just bringing all our resources with us. Exactly like you told us we need to do."

She looked back down the embankment at the Spur, the pavement gleaming wet in places and patchy with downed limbs. The Wrap's tires could grip once they made it to the flatter shoulder, she thought. They could drive and scan at the same time.

"Okay, but we're taking McCleary Road back. That's the direction he said he went."

Leo gestured vaguely west, toward the empty horizon. "Okay, okay. If he stuck to footpaths and skipped intersections, he'd steer through the low bowl where the old New Times Country Buffet was."

Hawthorne snorted, thinking of the long-ago defaced sign. "You mean the *End Times* Buffet?"

Leo gave a crooked smile. "Yeah, that one. Seems a little prophetic, doesn't it?"

She nodded but hesitated. She didn't want to leave the spot where Daniel had last been, but logic pushed past her immediate emotions.

Daniel wouldn't have left a note if he wasn't at least alive and mobile. Sitting around wasn't going to bring him or Wren back.

"All right," she said finally. "Let's get The Wrap on the road. I'll drive it, but fair warning, if I see footprints or anything, I'm stopping."

Leo nodded, stepping away so she could climb back aboard.

"Eli," she called as she reached the cab again, raising her voice. "We're taking the Spur down two miles and veering off to look. Daniel was trying to get to the police station on Dunn Street by way of McCleary Road."

He nodded and headed off to strategize with Leo.

The next thirty minutes blurred into a montage of sweat, mud, and cautious adrenaline. The embankment was slick and rutted, and more than once Hawthorne imagined the whole Wrap truck sliding sideways and taking her dreams of a smooth rescue with it. But Leo found tow straps in one of his truck's boxes, and between the three of them and a little careful pulling using the winch on Eli's truck, they got the heavy vehicle turned around and on the mostly-level pavement of the Spur.

Hawthorne took over from there.

She climbed into the driver's seat, wiped the condensation off the inside of the windshield with the cuff of her sleeve, and flicked on the ignition. The dash hummed to life, lights blinking amber as systems checked in. The Wrap's engine coughed once, then caught with a throaty rumble. Relief flooded her. The truck wasn't damaged and there was no good reason for it *not* to start, but she was grateful for every small miracle.

While Leo and Eli finished one last sweep around the area, checking some nearby cars for survivors (there were none), she did a quick inventory inside to get the truck ready for travel by double checking the locks on drawers, checking propane levels, securing bins and dry storage. A small container of sliced strawberries had come loose at some point, landing on the counter, and had gone soft and sour. She tossed it in the compost bin, then double-tied the latch. There wasn't much else to do, and she got back into the driver's seat, giving Leo a thumbs-up through the windshield.

Then they were off.

Leo took the lead in his facilities truck and Hawthorne followed in

The Wrap, the familiar jolt of its suspension slightly comforting under her hands. Eli brought up the rear in the second truck, far enough back to react if they needed to halt suddenly, close enough to guard for attacks.

They rolled south along the Spur, the road stretching ahead in broken gray lines and crumbled median signs, the damage from the storm looking worse the longer the day went, Hawthorne thought. Branches were down and there were still large puddles of water around, but still: no survivors, no zombies.

They passed a small blue hatchback left with both doors wide open, a pair of child's rain boots sitting neatly beside a puddle in front of it. Trash bags fluttered from a toppled utility trailer. A weathered billboard ahead read: "Where There's Hope, There's Calloway-Hayden A&M! Enroll for next semester!"

"Eyes focused," Hawthorne muttered, her hands tightening on the wheel as the convoy curved toward McCleary. The left onto McCleary was narrower than she'd remembered, choked with debris and abandoned vehicles. A fallen streetlight leaned against a delivery van like one drunk friend trying to help another home. But what caught Hawthorne's attention and made the hairs on the back of her neck rise was the path through the wreckage.

Someone had cleared it, although it was a haphazard job, obviously done on the fly.

But the way forward *had* been worked open, just enough for a vehicle to pass through in single file. A line of cars had been rolled or pushed aside, some with fresh scrape marks in the paint and wrenched-open doors as if someone had used brute force rather than tools. The road surface was patchy with branches and clusters of mud spatters. In the far distance, the roofline of the old buffet building poked above the trees like a forgotten crown.

Hawthorne slowed The Wrap to a crawl. She couldn't explain why, but everything in her body was telling her this wasn't good. Her foot hovered over the brake. Ahead of her, Leo's truck slowed down as well.

Hawthorne's gaze flicked toward the sidewalks. Front doors hung loose and a decorative pumpkin, oddly unseasonal and half-deflated, lay in a puddle under someone's mailbox. Curtains fluttered in broken windows. It was as quiet as their drive out, but it felt heavy, as if someone (something?) was watching.

She felt her chest tighten but kept The Wrap moving forward. And then, from one moment to another, she understood why a path had been cleared. As the old buffet's building came into view, she saw what were at least ten cars in the buffet's uneven, battered parking lot. One was an old farm-worthy flatbed truck with someone standing in the back, holding a gun.

The trucks rumbled slowly into the parking lot, gravel crunching beneath the tires, the vehicles rolling to a cautious stop just inside the haphazard car barricade that ringed the old buffet.

From her spot in The Wrap & Roll's cab, Hawthorne scanned the lot with narrow eyes. Most of the positioned vehicles were battered but not crushed, indicating that whoever moved them hadn't been working under fire. It was deliberate and defensive.

So was the kid with the hunting rifle in the back of the farm truck.

Seventeen, maybe. Baby-faced, thin arms holding the stock too close to his chest. His stance was more wary than aggressive, but Hawthorne knew one bad startle could still get everyone perforated. She gave him a slow, open-palmed wave through the windshield as Leo's truck came to a halt ten yards ahead.

After a thin, tense second, the boy nodded back. Just once.

Eli's truck halted behind Hawthorne's, and the parking lot settled into that same unnatural hush they'd come to dread. A single crow called from somewhere up in the rafters of the abandoned gas station across the street.

Then the buffet's side service door creaked open. A man stepped out, in his mid-thirties, square shoulders in a fatigue-style overshirt, clean but a little too pristine, like he insisted on looking put together even as society burned down. Hawthorne clocked the tucked-in shirt, the fashionable outdoor boots with minimal scuffing, and the faint but distinct JROTC-try-hard posture. His hair was close-cropped, and there was a radio clipped smartly to his belt. He didn't carry a weapon openly, which weirdly made her more cautious of him.

Leo slid out of his truck ahead, holding up both hands in a clear, non-threatening gesture. "We're not here to cause trouble," he called. "Just looking for someone."

The man nodded once but didn't smile. His eyes swept the convoy, stopping for a second too long on The Wrap & Roll truck before returning to Hawthorne, who leapt out of the cab and landed hard in the gravel.

"I'm looking for Daniel Phạm and his daughter Wren," Hawthorne said without preamble, stepping toward him just short of too fast. She kept her hands also visible, but her tone had an edge of urgency she could not hide. "He's the owner of that truck." She pointed at The Wrap & Roll.

The man didn't blink, but nodded amicably before he turned slightly, speaking over his shoulder toward the propped-open side door. "Tell Lacey to bring out Phạm and the kid."

His tone wasn't harsh, but it carried authority—the kind born from someone who's been giving orders for hours on end and hasn't once questioned if anyone else might have a better idea. Hawthorne was too familiar with the type.

A blur of motion inside the buffet flickered into view, and a girl, no older than twenty, stringy hair pulled under a baseball cap, probably related to the kid on the flat bed, ducked back into the shadows of the doorway.

"He's alive," the man said to Hawthorne, still in that professional-not-friendly tone. "And so's the girl. They got here this morning. Little scraped up, but they're breathing."

Hawthorne let herself breathe too. She hadn't even realized how tight her chest had gone. Around her, the tension eased slightly; Eli stepped around the rear of his truck and Leo moved up beside her, his stance easy but protective.

"I'm Reid Hollis," the man said next, holding out a hand like he was closing a deal. "Kinda been running things here since folks started showing up last night."

"Why here?

Reid just smiled jovially. "I asked the same thing. Was out looking for survivors last night and saw a bunch of people in the parking lot here. More been showin' up every few hours."

"You'd think people would go for a hospital, or at least Costco," Leo said, putting on a similarly blustery smile.

"You'd think," Reid said with a chuckle, crossing his arms.

Men sizing each other up, Hawthorne thought with chagrin.

A moment later, the old door creaked again, and Daniel emerged with a makeshift bandage at his temple and Wren tumbled out right behind him, clinging to her teddy bear backpack and skidding to a halt when she saw the trucks.

"*Uncle Hawk!*" she shouted gleefully, immediately launching herself across the gravel parking lot.

It hit Hawthorne like both a punch and a blessing at once to hear the quirky nickname Wren had saddled her with when she first learned to talk. Hawthorne broke into a run then, scooping Wren up into her arms, nearly crying from the sheer relief of solid, squirmy, six-year-old life. "Hey, noodle-brain," she whispered, burying her face in the girl's shoulder. "I'm so happy that you're okay."

Wren leaned back in Hawthorne's arms slightly, her small fingers gripping tight to the collar of Hawthorne's coat as her expression shifted. "Dad says we have to stay here where it's safe," she said with a pout, scrunching her nose. "But I'm tired of snack bars."

Hawthorne managed a smile, and gently smoothed down Wren's hair, but her pulse was still hammering with relief. She would never have forgiven herself if something had happened to Wren. "I'm sure your dad can make a sandwich now that you've got The Wrap back," she said lightly, trying for a normal tone and gesturing at the food truck behind her.

She set Wren down as Daniel caught up, breathing heavy with a tight smile and focused eyes.

"Thanks for the truck," he said in a low voice, eyes flicking toward Reid. "You found it?"

"More like it waited for us," she replied. "Got your note. Good thinking."

Before he could say more, Leo stepped up beside them, nodding toward the spread of vehicles in the lot.

"There's gotta be what—fifty, sixty people here?" he said, voice low.

"More keep showing up," Reid said, joining them. "Got a few

yesterday evening, almost two dozen overnight. People driving for safety or looking for loved ones see other survivors and pull in. Simple as that. We have to stay together in an emergency like this."

He crossed his arms, glancing toward the boarded-up buffet like it was a fortress instead of a remnant of a time gone by with faded murals of cornucopias peeling from the corners.

"This place has visibility and just enough shelter to feel safe," Reid continued. "Better than strip malls or old gyms. The boarded windows help, but without electricity it can get a bit spooky."

"Safety in numbers," Leo said, thoughtful.

"Or the illusion of safety," Daniel muttered. He knelt to check the strap on Wren's shoe but didn't look up.

Reid nodded at Leo, not having heard Daniel. "I was getting ready to propose we swap out with someplace that has electric, since the grid is clearly still running." He waved toward the street corner, where the stoplight was dutifully directing non-existent traffic. "Maybe a big box store; it would have supplies and limited entryways."

Leo nodded thoughtfully while Eli stood by. Hawthorne only half-heard the conversation, her gaze wandering back to the open door that Wren and Daniel had come out of, to see a few people joining them.

Hawthorne scanned the huddle at the buffet entrance, faces pale under overcast light, eyes wide and searching in every direction but toward each other. No blood. No bandages. Just the quick, shallow breathing of people who had run until they couldn't run anymore, then clung to the first place filled with people who weren't zombies.

A woman cradled a Chihuahua in her denim jacket. An older man in paint-streaked overalls clutched a gallon of spring water like it was gold. A teenager stood half-hidden behind a cracked post, watching her group but not stepping closer, like trust was another storm bearing down from the horizon.

They weren't hurt, but they were all obviously stunned and traumatized, their strength fraying like old yarn. It really felt like the day after a tornado, only without all the news crews crawling around.

They had zombies instead.

Reid's voice carried over her shoulder, still polished and pragmatic. "They came from all different directions, back roads, farm turn-offs, apartments that flooded. Some talk about schools locking up too fast, some about hospitals turning people away..." He trailed off, squinting as if trying to decode something just out of reach.

Hawthorne's mind snapped back to the guttered cars along the Spur, the stroller, the blinking hazard lights. She thought suddenly of Lincoln High, where her old boyfriend Matt taught social studies, and of the two nursing homes on Briar Hill. Of how no one here had said they came from those directions, and how Reid hadn't mentioned either one.

"You think the ones still out there don't know where to go," she said flatly.

Leo inclined his head, the barest nod.

"They aren't looking for shelters," she went on, her voice quiet but steady. "They're just looking for other people. This place..." She glanced up at the stained awning, one of the boards above the door still faintly reading 'COUNTRY BUFFET' in peeled vinyl letters. "They just saw cars in the lot and followed the humans."

Reid also nodded but looked at her questioningly.

"The zombies are out there," she added, more to herself than anyone else. "Watching the roads and waiting for who knows what. Meanwhile, there are probably hundreds, even thousands of people just locked up and waiting for calvary to come bail us out."

Leo looked sideways at her, worry flickering in his expression.

"They're clustered here by instinct," he finally said. "Follow the movement, follow each other. It's just a different kind of herding."

"Well, we have to save them!" Hawthorne said loudly. Dan had a conflicted look on his face, and Eli was his usual stoic self, but Leo shook his head.

"Right now, we are trying to save who we can and get back to the agri center. Remember what Mendez said? No side trips or heroics."

"People need our help! These people! People trapped in schools, hospitals, laundromats!"

"Laundromats?" Daniel muttered.

She turned on him. "You know what I mean!"

He held up his hands in surrender. "I do! But, lean, dark, and handsome there has a point."

Leo blushed. “Leo Foxx. I’m just...uh, Leo Foxx.”

“Nice to meet you. Anyway, can we just get The Wrap to the agri center so I can see my sister?”

“We can’t just let them sit out there,” she said, louder than she intended, her stomach twisting helplessly.

Leo turned toward her, brows already drawn. “We’re not letting them do anything. We’re making sure *we* don’t die trying to help them.”

She shot him a look, a quick flare of disbelief. “What about Lincoln High? And Brekke Elementary? They’re across the street from each other. That’s over five hundred kids if the buildings were even half full when the storm hit.”

Her voiçe didn’t shake, but her heart was pounding. She felt helpless again, like she did watching her father die. Watching her mother grieve. Watching her future evaporate on a food truck griddle.

“Those places will be locked down and probably barricaded. If the shufflers haven’t gotten in, their own people might not let us near the place,” Leo said quietly.

“Then we knock louder!” she shot back. “We drive up, we yell, we—”

“What if we can’t protect them?” Leo asked, cutting her off, his tone finally cracking, just for a moment. “What if we bring the danger right to them? You think we’re a cavalry, but two trucks and a food van don’t make us zombie-proof, Hawthorne!”

Her name out of his mouth like that—direct, short—felt like something snapping in the dust-dry air between them.

“We’re going back to the agri center,” he added with the weariness of someone trying to convince a tide not to rise. “We’ll plan better from there.”

“You mean *you’ll* plan,” Hawthorne said. The bitterness slid in before she had a chance to strangle it. “We’ll wait, again, just like everyone else is waiting. And while we wait, more people die.”

A few voices behind them muttered to each other. Eli continued to stay out of it, his arms folded, face as unreadable as slate, and Daniel had stepped inside with Wren again, giving them space—or escaping it, she thought with chagrin, knowing how he hated confrontation.

“You think I don’t know that? We all know that!” He gestured at the people walking out of the old buffet, drawn by the noise. "The agri center is the safest place in town right now, but it can't hold an entire city's population!"

Before Hawthorne could argue, Eli uncrossed his arms and put his hands on his hips. "Dr. Foxx is right. We need to get these people to safety first. If they want to come, they can follow us, but we need to go soon."

It was all he said, but it was enough. Reid, who had been watching the exchange like a tennis match, nodded. Hawthorne raised her hands in defeat but stomped off, circling around the back of the building in hopes of walking off her frustration. It wasn't that they were wrong and she was right, but that they were *all* right, and there was no "good" choice to make.

The gravel shifted under Hawthorne's boots as she rounded the corner of the building, her pulse still thrumming from the argument, the back of her neck tight and hot. She wasn't sure if she was angrier at Leo or herself, but knew the answer was "both." The late-morning light was thin and golden, and back there, away from the others congregating at the front, the city was quiet again. The usual flow of people and traffic was gone, just the murmurings of everyone up front drifting through the air. The shadows stretched longer across the patchy asphalt of what had once been the employee lot. It smelled faintly of moss and wet asphalt.

The lot sloped slightly into a low dip of overgrowth that continued into knee-high grass tangled through with the rusted bones of what used to be a tiny faux castle under the trees. It was all that remained of the mini-golf course that had lived there before the buffet even opened but had closed when Hawthorne was a child. It was all wild now. She stopped for a deep breath and watched a squirrel dart across an upturned cone. Somewhere to her left, a pigeon burst from the underbrush, wings loud in the hush.

And then she saw Wren.

She was a small blur of a pink hoodie and a bear backpack, bobbing like a flag, sprinting down the slope and vanishing between two overgrown hedges.

"Wren!" Hawthorne barked, her voice cracking in the still air.

If anything, Wren sped up.

Hawthorne's blood chilled in panic, and she ran. Down the slope, into the old mini golf ruins, her boots slipping a little on wet grass, mud, and undergrowth. Her breath came fast, shallow, a counter-thrum to the panic rising as she pushed through vines and kudzu, calling louder, "WREN!"

Branches clawed at her jacket and a low, broken fence snagged briefly at her shin, slowing her stride. The green space opened wider the farther in she went, the trees older here, ambient sound muffled by moss and ivy hanging like theater curtains.

Then she spotted her.

Wren stood just ahead beside a crooked stone bridge that was half-swallowed by mold. She wasn't moving, but she was looking at something with her eyes wide, mouth slightly open.

"Wren, what are you doing?" Hawthorne asked, her voice low now but slicing through the air as she approached.

The girl didn't turn. "I saw him," she said simply.

Hawthorne's breath caught. "Who?" she whispered, though she already knew.

Wren cast a glance at her over one shoulder, small and earnest. "Pops."

Hawthorne stopped a few feet away, her boots planting hard in the loamy earth. The shadows under the old trees curled inward like they were listening too. "You saw your other dad?" she asked gently, trying to keep her voice calm even though her stomach knotted.

Wren nodded, eyes still fixed on the gnarled edge of the overgrown mini-golf castle just beyond the bridge. Her hands were tight at her sides, not afraid exactly... more like filled with a purpose too big to hold. "He was all shiny around the edges. Like... like he was wrapped in fairy lights."

Hawthorne blinked. "What?"

"He glowed," Wren said simply, like it was the most obvious thing in the world. "Around his hair and hands. And I could see through him a little bit. He waved and smiled at me." Her voice faltered only slightly.

It hit Hawthorne like a dropped pane of glass.

Last she knew, Adrien was alive, somewhere safe, not here. He worked at the university in administration but had just recently moved out of the house he shared with Daniel and Wren in preparation for divorce. There was no reason to think he'd—

The thought cut off.

No more communications signals. No phone calls. No anything from the college since before the storm came crashing in. She realized with a jolt that she hadn't thought about how long it had been since anyone had gotten a text or message from anyone.

"Adrien…" Hawthorne said aloud, but more to herself.

"He was right there," Wren said, stepping closer to the old bridge's crumbling edge. "I know it was him."

"Wren." Hawthorne's voice sharpened. She moved forward, placing a hand on the girl's shoulder. Wren resisted slightly, her body humming with something Hawthorne recognized from herself: pure, desperate belief in the impossible. "Listen to me. Whoever or whatever you saw, we need to go back. Right now."

"But I have to find him!"

Hawthorne crouched, trying to make her face level with Wren's. "We'll ask your dad what he's heard, okay? Maybe your pops is somewhere safe."

Wren's eyes went wet around the corners. "He wouldn't leave me," she said softly.

Hawthorne's heart clenched. She reached out more firmly, both hands resting on Wren's arms now. "I know, kiddo. I know he wouldn't," Hawthorne said, trying to thread calm into every word despite the sudden pressure behind her ribs. "But right now, we need to go talk to your dad. You're not alone. He's not either."

Wren bit her lip, her eyes darting once more toward the place where she'd seen the glowing figure. Her voice dropped to almost nothing. "But she looked so real."

"I believe you." Hawthorne didn't flinch as she said it. It was the easiest truth in the world, even if there was a lot of omission going on. "But even if he's trying to tell us something, I don't think he wants you running off into the woods alone to find out what it is."

That worked. Wren's shoulder sagged just a sliver, her body leaning into Hawthorne's without quite meaning to. Hawthorne guided her gently around, back toward the overgrown path. "We can come looking together," she said, "but *later*. When it's safer."

Wren nodded, just once.

They were halfway up the slope when the first scream tore through the quiet. It came jagged from the front of the buffet—high and raw and punctuated. Hawthorne froze.

Another shout followed it. Then two voices overlapping, one barking orders and the unmistakable thudding crunch of a heavy body hitting metal. Wren clutched Hawthorne's hand instantly, her tiny fingers digging into Hawthorne's palm.

Zombies. It had to be. The shouting. The chaos. They'd been drawn by the noise, or maybe always watching and waiting from the other side of the trees. Either way, they were here.

"It's okay," Hawthorne said, already yanking Wren into her arms, standing into a running crouch. "It's going to be okay. Hold on tight."

They came quietly, just shadows at first, then shapes with that stomach-churning gait that never looked like it should keep a body upright. One limped between the collapsed fiberglass windmill and what used to be hole eight's pirate ship. Another lurched past the mossy stone mushroom, mouth open like it was tasting the overgrown air.

Three... four... five. Not a big crowd yet, but wrong in that visceral way that made Hawthorne's every nerve want to climb out of her skin.

Her breath caught. "Oh no. No, no, no."

Wren was still in her arms, clinging tight. Hawthorne cursed softly and spun on her heel. The parking lot exit they'd come through now sat under dusk-shadowed trees... and more shufflers, strange figures weaving through the brush like stringless marionettes, invisible until they weren't. One tripped over the curb and half-fell, then slowly forced itself upright again with the jerky tenacity of something that didn't care if bones bent wrong.

The way back to the buffet was swarming.

"Okay," she whispered, more to herself than Wren. "We zigzag."

She bolted for the edge of the lot and cut hard left. Wren didn't scream, gods bless her, but she clung like a baby koala, letting Hawthorne run with all the adrenaline her gangly arms could provide.

Coming around the back of an old payday loan storefront, she saw motion up the street toward the buffet again, dozens of shapes, some joining from side alleys, others emerging haphazardly from between parked cars. The half-collapsed gas station canopy groaned unsettlingly under its own weight, punctuating the danger they were in.

"Too many," Hawthorne muttered, skidding into a narrow side street. "Way too many."

She dropped behind a rusted trash bin and crouched in what smelled like spilled beer. Her breath came hard and quick, and she shushed Wren gently as the girl whimpered into her jacket.

They weren't just heading to the buffet, they were converging. Like the whole pocket of the city was exhaling rot and fury all at once.

They had stirred up some kind of attention, too emotional, too loud, too much all at once—she wasn't sure, but she knew it wasn't coincidence. Fortunately, they seemed focused on the buffet and not on her and Wren.

Just then, she heard the heavy noise of a truck engine. The engine snarled like an over-caffeinated kitten as the squat, bubblegum-pink van barreled around the corner. Hawthorne blinked. Cutting through the wreckage of the intersection like it was just another Monday morning came a stubby, ancient, converted van absolutely plastered in pastel decals. Cartoon marshmallows. An anxious boba cup with sleepy eyes. Sparkling lattes with wings. Across the driver's side in a looping, aggressively whimsical font was the name:

PERKY UPPY.

It skidded to a halt just in front of her. The side window cranked down manually (because of course it was manual) revealing a petite girl with a frilly lavender top and jet-black hair tied in two messy buns. Her cat-eye sunglasses in neon green were pushed up onto her head, and her cheeks were flushed with either overexertion or sheer manic energy.

"GET IN!" the girl shouted, flinging the passenger door open. "I have oatmilk, Bluetooth, and three prayers left to Saint Dwayne the Rock Johnson!"

Hawthorne didn't hesitate. She heaved Wren through the door and scrambled in after her, slamming the door shut as the van squealed into motion again. Outside, a pair of shufflers turned toward the sound and disappeared behind them in a blur of rust and moving grass.

"I'm Andy," the girl offered, eyes glued to the road but somehow managing to steer one-handed while flipping three switches on some kind of panel covered in frog stickers. The interior smelled like cinnamon and cheap espresso.

"Hawthorne," she gasped, breath finally finding an anchor. "And this is Wren. You just—holy crap—you just saved us."

"Hah!" Andy grinned wide enough that it nearly blinded. "Knew I saw someone small and someone big doing very un-casual running. Rule number two of the zombie apocalypse—save the kid." She smiled at Wren. "Welcome to the Perky Uppy coffee cart!"

Wren stared at her, wide eyed, her breath hiccupping but small and steady. "Do you have hot cocoa?"

CHAPTER 8

Clairemont Welcomes You

Hawthorne gripped the door handle in one hand and stabilized Wren with the other as the Perky Uppy hit a pothole and bounced like a carnival ride someone forgot to secure. Cardamom-scented air and the faint remnant of espresso filled the cabin in sweet, bizarre contrast to the chaos they'd just escaped.

Wren wiggled in her lap like a very small, determined squirrel. "I'm not buckled in," she announced, indignant, for the third time.

"Well, we're in a cupcake on wheels," Hawthorne muttered. "There isn't exactly a five-point harness option. Just hold on."

Andy, one hand on the wheel and the other reaching past a line of dangling anime keychains for what looked like a bag of mini marshmallows, didn't break her focus. "Here, marshmallows will soften the impact." She handed the bag to Wren, who looked at it skeptically.

"Look, we need to go to the old buffet—" Hawthorne tried again.

"Flavored syrup costs extra, and I do not go back for exes or zombies," Andy cut in, eyes flicking to the rear-view mirror, where more shufflers were becoming visible behind them like slow, horrible parade floats. "That whole area is crawling, like, actually crawling with zombies!"

"We have people there," Hawthorne snapped. "Wren's dad among them! I need you to turn this pink Xanax nightmare around."

Andy's hands tightened around the steering wheel wrapped in pink silicone espresso bean decals. There was a micro-pause that was almost imperceptible. Someone who wasn't riding a thin veil of panic might've missed it, but Hawthorne felt it like a misstep on a staircase.

Andy's voice didn't change tone when she finally said, "No can do. Not until we get somewhere safe, and I mean safe with emphasis, italics, and possibly glitter. You're welcome, by the way, for the rescue."

"I don't know you, so this might be out of left field, but what are you not telling me?" Hawthorne asked sharply. Wren had gone quiet in her lap, realizing that the adults were arguing.

Andy didn't answer right away. She blinked hard, then she hit the turn signal out of habit and blew out a breath like she was exhaling out of the bottom of her boots as she made the turn through the torn-up intersection, where one stoplight was sagging to one side.

"I'm not telling you because I figured you'd try to stop me," she admitted. "And I don't have time for that. I won't leave you by the side of the road, I'm not a jerk, but I can't be your taxi. I got a text, okay? This morning. Somehow it got through."

"A text?" Hawthorne repeated, squinting.

Andy finally peeled her eyes off the road for half a second to glance sideways. "From my little brother, Jules. He's ten. Said he's trapped in his school with three teachers and a bunch of other kids. A bunch of the staff and even a few of the kids turned zombie during the freak storm, so the surviving teachers have them all in lockdown in a few classrooms."

Hawthorne went still.

"He says the teachers boarded things up when they could, but they're low on food and meds and everyone's scared," Andy continued, her voice going flatter. "Our parents are on another stupid cruise. They aren't coming for him."

Wren's little hand found one of Hawthorne's jacket buttons and held on.

"That's why I can't turn around," Andy said.

Wren, inexplicably serious, looked up at her. "He's your brother."

"Yeah."

"And ohana means family, and family means—"

Both Andy and Hawthorne automatically helped her finish the famous phrase from *Lilo & Stitch*: "No one gets left behind!"

Andy pumped her fist and laughed. "Yeah!"

Hawthorne leaned her head back against the seat, realizing she had lost the battle. "Which school?"

"Oh. Clairemont Middle."

Clairemont Middle wasn't far, sitting by itself in the middle of an older area of town. It used to be the high school, back in the 1980s, and could hold at most about two hundred kids. Hawthorne's gut twisted. "There might be hundreds of people still alive in those buildings," she said quietly, already knowing that any plan she came up with would sound like madness to someone else. But it didn't make it less true.

Andy nodded, more subdued than she'd been since they met. "Yeah. That's why I'm going, even if I have to drive through a marching band of corpse-walkers to get there."

Hawthorne half-smiled, fighting her way through feelings of terror and determination. She had been the one to argue for immediate rescue runs, after all.

"Well, I'm not letting you do that alone. And we're coming up with a real plan, not just a caffeine-fueled joyride into a reanimated city block."

Andy side-eyed her. "Do you make all your big life decisions mid-kidnap slash coffee cruise?"

"Hi, I'm Hawthorne Porter, head chef of The Gourmet Grinder," she said with a grin she did not feel.

"I knew I knew you! I love that place!" Andy grinned back.

Hawthorne chuckled, soft and uneven, the sound spilling out before she could stop it. "So," she said, glancing down at Wren and brushing a bit of leaf from her hoodie, "Step one is... not dying. That's the bones of it."

Andy gave a theatrical nod. "Firm foundation."

"And step two," she continued, slowly now, "is figuring out how to get into Clairemont without making it a buffet line—zombie version. Maybe do some scouting first."

"Mm. Less 'drive up in an americano panic van,' more 'ninja espresso infiltration,'" Andy nodded. "Got it."

"Were you a lit major?" Hawthorne asked, squinting at her.

"Close. I dropped out of the pre-med program."

That explained a lot, Hawthorne thought.

Wren gave a thoughtful hum as she set the marshmallow bag onto her lap and picked one out with determined ceremony. "I think we need walkie-talkies," she said seriously. "Like *Paw Patrol.*"

Andy glanced in the rear-view mirror. "She's got good instincts."

Hawthorne tapped a finger against her temple. "We need more than that. I think we need Leo, and Eli, and the trucks."

Andy raised her eyebrows but didn't look away from the street. "Oh? Leo's the cavalry?"

"He's the cavalry," Hawthorne confirmed. "But also painfully practical, which this plan could use. And if I show up with this idea alone, he might just feed me to the zombies himself."

Andy snorted. "Tell him it's for the children."

"I would if I could," Hawthorne said. "But more importantly, this one's dad is probably looking for her and freaked out."

Andy grimaced but nodded. "I get it, I get it. FINE! I'll take you back, but then I'm going for my brother!"

"We can call Dad!" Wren announced like she had just solved world hunger.

"No, we can't. Phone service has gone a bit wacky." Hawthorne sighed as Andy started to turn around.

"We can! I told you I got the talkie!" Wren yanked on the zipper of her backpack and pulled out a walkie talkie. Dan had bought them a while back when his marriage was still strong and he and his husband would take turns walking infant Wren during food truck hours.

"Oh, my God, Wren! You rock!" Hawthorne said with a smile.

Andy had already course-corrected yet again to head to the school while Hawthorne turned on the walkie talkie, pleased to see that it had about eighty percent charge left. It crackled alive with a burst of static. Then a familiar, desperate voice melted through the fuzz like it had been screaming across dimensions to reach her.

"Wren? Wren! Are you out there? It's Dad! I need to know you're okay, baby. Please answer. Please answer."

Hawthorne nearly dropped the radio in sheer adrenaline, fumbling with the side button. Wren scrambled to sit upright in her lap.

"Dan! Dan, it's okay, she's with me!" Hawthorne said into the walkie, her voice already climbing.

"Oh, thank God." Dan's voice went soft with relief. "Are you okay? Is she hurt?"

"We're fine," Hawthorne said. "Scared and covered in leaves, but fine. She ran after—there was a... it doesn't matter. A little chase, a little detour. I'll explain later. We're in a van. A barista van. The Perky Uppy?"

A pause. Then: "Andy's van?" he asked, like he already hated himself for knowing that.

"That's the one."

"Great," Dan muttered, then said loudly, "Thank you, Andy!"

Andy reached across the van's cabin to give the walkie a firm pat with two fingers. "You're welcome! Had no idea the spawn was yours!"

Hawthorne exhaled hard, then pressed the radio back to her mouth. "Dan, listen. We heard screaming, and by the time we turned back, the buffet was crawling. We couldn't get to you."

"They were slow enough that we got almost everyone into cars. Eli is leading everyone to the agri center. Well, except Leo and me, I wouldn't leave without... Never mind! You both on the way to Hayden?"

"Ah, about that. No."

"What? No? What do you mean, no? You have my daughter, Hawk!"

"I know, and I've still got her! Andy was on her way to Clairemont Middle; her brother's trapped there. I can't ask her to leave him behind while we roll to safety."

There was a pause. "Wait. What? You're going *where?*"

"Clairemont," she said again, firmer now. "Your daughter is with me. Safe. Look, your truck is mobile, remember? If you head out now, you can catch up to us."

"Are you kidding me?" Dan hissed. "I just got her back, and you want me to run her headlong into a school lockdown slash zombie siege with the Bubblegum Avenger?!"

Andy gave a mock salute, clearly not offended.

"We've got a plan," Hawthorne continued quickly. "Okay, no, we don't have a plan yet," she admitted. "But we are making one. A better one than 'sit tight and hope.'" She paused. "Dan, it's her ten-year-old brother."

She could hear Dan exhale tightly through the speaker. Probably pacing in half-circles in The Wrap's tiny crew area, one hand in his hair and the other clenched like it was trying to crush panic into dust.

"I'm coming," he said finally, low and taut. "Don't do anything rash until I catch up."

"Got it," Hawthorne said, relief blooming so fast her hands trembled. "Drive careful."

"Drive smart," Dan corrected, in the bone-deep tone only parents and survivors seemed to share now. "And don't let her out of your sight."

"Not happening," Hawthorne promised.

But then another voice cut in, sputtered through static with the crisp bite of tension: "Hawthorne."

Leo.

Of course he'd wrestled the radio away the second Dan cracked. There was something in Leo's voice that sounded like disappointment braided under worry, the kind of simmer she recognized from working the food truck when she had six fatty burgers on the grill and no splatter screen.

"I swear to every law of physics," Leo said, "if you've dragged her into this on instinct alone—"

"I didn't drag anyone!" Hawthorne snapped. "She was already going!"

"The kid ran off for no reason, and now instead of coming back, you're making a detour into goddamn apocalypse high school?"

"It's a middle school," Andy said off to the side, primly offended.

Hawthorne ignored both of them and pressed the walkie back to her mouth. "I made a call. Because someone has to."

"You don't even know what conditions are like," Leo pressed on. "What if the school's overrun? What if it's not secure or, hell, what if your presence makes it worse for them? For the kids already hiding?"

"I know that's possible," Hawthorne admitted, her throat tight.

"But I also know we can't wait for the 'right time' to help. When we can help, we help! We can't keep playing it safe and calling it strategy."

There was a pause. A long one. On the other end of the signal, maybe Leo was trying to decide if she was brave or just reckless enough to get them all killed.

"You're doing that thing again," he said finally, carefully, "where you act like taking the hardest, most self-sacrificing road is somehow the clearest choice."

Hawthorne blinked.

Leo continued, voice roughened by static but unmistakably raw. "I know what you're doing, Hawthorne. You're trying to make it count. I know it's not just about Andy's brother or those kids. It's about every person we didn't get to soon enough already."

Heat rose in her cheeks, her hand clenching the radio just a fraction tighter.

"And yeah," he added, "maybe I don't want anyone else to die either. But I especially don't want it to be you."

That last part rang out so sharply that for a moment, the silence on their end wasn't just quiet, it was patience and concern and unspoken emotions.

Andy let out a delicate, theatrical "oooooooh" from the driver's seat without looking away from the road.

"I am literally sitting here," Dan said over the channel, as if offended on philosophical grounds.

"Uncle Hawk?" Wren piped up, still nestled in Hawthorne's lap. "Is Leo mad?"

Hawthorne sighed, tucking an arm securely around her and pressing the talk button. "He's just doing what he always does, sweetie. Thinking sixteen steps ahead while I try not to get eaten."

"I'd feel much better," Leo returned dryly, "if one of those steps included not launching an extracurricular rescue mission based on a text message and a barista's caffeine high."

"I'm a very skilled barista, okay?" Andy chimed in, offended.

"We're already halfway there," Hawthorne said, softly this time. "I'll be careful. We'll find out what's happening at Clairemont and get the hell back to you."

Another pause.

And finally, in a tired, resigned voice that made her chest ache, Leo answered. "Then don't forget," he said, "No hero moves. You play it safe."

Hawthorne swallowed hard. "Copy that." The channel clicked off, leaving only the low purr of the Perky Uppy cutting through the shell of a broken city.

Andy turned the wheel with a smooth flick and peered at her sidelong. "You okay?" she asked.

"No," Hawthorne admitted. Wren snuggled closer, obviously trying to comfort her.

"So, what are the chances of both Leo and Dan showing up?" Andy asked casually.

"High. Very high. He might even call Eli to circle around and meet up once he's led the caravan to Hayden."

"Eli?" Andy frowned. The van rattled over a cracked patch of pavement, and Andy's frown deepened, as if her brain was filing away the name "Eli" under the category of Things To Worry About Later.

"Eli Dale," Hawthorne confirmed, shifting Wren in her lap as the girl finally nibbled a marshmallow with the weight of a war ration. "Tall. Looks like he could wrestle a bear and apologize after. Forestry student. Lowkey poetry nerd. Carries a shotgun like it's a purse."

Andy blinked. "Wait. Guy with the square jaw and hair like a shampoo commercial, but he gets bashful around dogs?"

"That's the one," Hawthorne muttered, then added, "How on earth do you remember that?"

"I never forget an order, and I never forget a face. He's, uh, got a nice face. And he likes caramel latte with extra foam."

"Isn't that just a cappuccino?"

"Heathen," Andy muttered under her breath as she navigated around more empty cars.

"I didn't know he got bashful around dogs," Hawthorne said as a peace offering.

"Oh yeah," Andy said, now vaguely distracted with the mental image. "Last spring, I saw him try to pet one at the civic fair and he looked like he was asking it for prom. Offered the dog his full name and everything."

Hawthorne couldn't help it, she laughed. A short, startled sound that cracked something open in her chest in the best possible way. Wren giggled in tandem, though mostly at the word "prom."

The van hit another bump and Andy steered around an abandoned SUV without bothering to slow. Outside the window, the buildings grew more residential—familiar trees with storm-tattered limbs, the occasional mailbox half-ripped from the ground. The kind of neighborhood that, two days ago, might've been full of kids on scooters, teens sulking on porches, teachers coming home with takeout and aching feet.

Now it was just shadows and the whip sound of wind through loose siding.

"We're close," she commented. Andy tapped the dashboard like it owed her a favor. "Couple more turns. Five minutes if the road stays clear. Nine if we don't hit anything that used to breathe."

Hawthorne nodded, gazing out the window. Her nerves coiled tighter. The street sloped downward as they neared the school zone, and from the higher incline, she could see the squat red-brick shape of Clairemont Middle rising behind a narrow hedgerow and a sagging iron fence. Its windows were dark. A peeled banner hung by one corner above the double doors, fluttering like a slow-motion SOS: "CLAIREMONT WELCOMES YOU!"

Nothing about it felt welcoming now.

Andy rolled the Perky Uppy to a stop behind a box truck, its back doors flung wide revealing empty crates and a single boot. She killed the engine in a quick, practiced flick.

Silence collapsed around them.

Wren pressed closer to the window, face round and pale in the glass. "Where are the cars?"

Hawthorne did a slow sweep of the lot and the block beyond. "They're here. Just scattered. Looks like a few made a run for it, at least."

They all sat silently, looking around for a minute. The zombies were easy to miss at first because they didn't move. They stood like crooked signposts around the school's perimeter, just beyond the playground fence and beneath the leafless oaks. Not bunched up together and not reaching out for anything.

One leaned slightly against a lamppost, head tilted to the side like it'd fallen asleep standing. Another stood at the edge of the baseball diamond, arms limp, chin dropped forward as if staring at an invisible mound.

Andy whispered, "Okay, I've worked morning shift during parents weekend, and this is creepier."

Hawthorne nodded once, slow and tense. "I don't like how still they are."

"They're waiting," Wren said suddenly, voice thin and quiet.

Hawthorne turned sharply. "What?"

"They're not confused," Wren said. "They're waiting for something." There was no humor. No fear, either. Just recognition, like she was remembering something she was told.

Hawthorne stared harder at the field again and felt the wrongness humming across the air like a power line. The hairs on her arms lifted. She fumbled for the walkie-talkie and pressed the call button. "Leo. This is Hawthorne. We're at Clairemont. There's something—" She paused, watching one of the zombies slowly, mechanically tilt its head toward the sound of a birdcall overhead then tilt it back. "—something's different here," she finished.

Static answered for a few seconds too long before the walkie crackled and coughed up Leo's voice, edged with static and urgency. "What do you mean 'different'?"

"They're not acting like the others," Hawthorne whispered, eyes locked on the parking lot. "They're not just shuffling around, following people to where the action is. It's more like they're *stationed*, watching the building like bouncers who forgot their job."

Andy leaned forward on the steering wheel, lips thinned. "Post-apocalyptic meet and greet?"

Hawthorne shot her a look, but even she appreciated the effort beneath the sarcasm. "They're entirely not blocked off by fences either. Which means they could go in but haven't." She hesitated. "That's not nothing."

Leo's voice returned, clipped but steady. "We're a few blocks back. We should be with you in ten."

The walkie fell quiet. The van seemed too loud even without the engine running.

Andy twisted in her seat, grabbing her thermal mug from the cupholder and tossing it back like a shot of whiskey. "All right," she said, mouth full of steam and determination. "Here's the rest of the plan. We don't just sit here."

"You're thinking recon," Hawthorne said.

"Two-minute sweep," Andy replied. "Low and quiet. Side entrance is probably closest. We look, we listen, we bail back to the Perky Uppy if things go sideways."

Hawthorne nodded. "Wren stays."

The girl crossed her arms. "You both talk too much. I should go."

Hawthorne grinned despite herself. "Nice try, Paw Patrol. But if you're our communications center, you gotta hold the fort." She tapped the walkie. "Your job's important."

Wren seemed to consider that for a long second, then finally nodded, very official. "Okay. But you have to tell me everything after."

"You'll get the full debrief," Hawthorne said, then waved toward the side lot. "Lock the doors, okay? Now! Let's go."

They popped the doors quietly, trying not to disturb the dead things standing in their unnatural stillness. The hinges on Hawthorne's side gave a tiny squeak, not loud but enough to make her wince. She stepped out onto old, cracked pavement, slipping briefly on a half-crushed soda can before catching herself on the van's side mirror. Andy joined her a heartbeat later, crouched low, holding what looked like a micro-foam whip nozzle like it was her preferred self-defense weapon.

The air smelled of ozone and stale cafeteria meatloaf.

They stayed to the edge of the lot and crept through the sparsely spaced rows of parked cars, ducking low behind a faded maroon minivan. Just ahead, Clairemont's side entrance came into view, a gray service door with a paper sign taped to it, fluttering despite having three strips of tape holding it down.

Hawthorne squinted. "Back entrance. Probably to the kitchen," she whispered.

Andy nodded. "I've snuck into a lot of kitchens." At Hawthorne's glare, she held up her hands. "For valid reasons!"

The zombies by the main fence didn't move, just stood there barely twitching as the breeze nudged their clothes. Hawthorne felt a prickle climb her spine. Wren had said they were waiting, but for what? A noise, a smell, a person?

They reached the side door after one final sprint crouch, Andy practically pressing her ear to the metal. Then she pointed to the sign. In crooked Sharpie, someone had scrawled:

LOCKED BUT TRY KITCHEN WINDOW LEFT OPEN FOR LOU.

- Ms. Trisha

Hawthorne blinked. "Lou?"

Andy grinned. "I am now Lou."

"What happened to 'two-minute sweep and back to the van'?" Hawthorne hissed.

"Do what you want, I'm going in to find Josh."

Hawthorne mimed throttling her, but Andy simply ducked out of her reach. She backtracked a few feet and scanned left and pointed up. A wide kitchen window, raised just high enough off the wall to make entry inconvenient, but not impossible. The glass had been propped up by an old thermos. Someone had draped a dish towel over the sill.

Andy muttered, "Thank you, Ms. Trisha." Then to Hawthorne, "Boost me, and I'll pull you in."

"Hold on one second," Hawthorne said and went to peek back out at the parking lot. Wren was in the driver's seat, looking out the windshield intently. She waved when she saw Hawthorne, who pointed at herself then the building. Wren nodded and before Hawthorne could shriek in terror she opened the door, hopped out, and sprinted for Hawthorne.

A couple of zombies clocked her movement but stayed still, almost as if they thought she was the wrong person. Maybe she was.

Hawthorne grabbed her and held her close, wanting to yell at her, but then remembered she would rather have Wren close by than alone. And, she had promised Daniel not to lose sight of his daughter.

"Are we breaking in?" Wren whispered in excitement.

"Ohana!" Andy said, making it sound like a war cry despite the fact that she was whispering too.

Andy crawled in with no issues after a boost from Hawthorne, who then passed Wren through the window. Hawthorne followed far less gracefully, although she was happy not to twist her ankle on the landing inside.

Inside, the air was warmer, and weirdly normal. The smell of overcooked spaghetti lingered beneath the sterile tang of sanitizer and tray soap. Hawthorne immediately scanned for movement, but the kitchen was quiet and dark, the overhead florescent lighting turned off. The only light came from high slats behind them, angled dull and gray with settling dust.

Rows of industrial ovens and warming carts stood dark and unplugged, the metal surfaces battered from use but clean enough to reflect the faint light filtering through slatted blinds. Trays were stacked neatly by the prep sinks, and a collection of milk cartons stood forgotten on a rolling cart against the far wall, sweating slowly into condensation puddles.

Andy headed for one of the internal doors, which looked like it led to a hallway. "Okay. So far, low on zombie content but high with the extremely nostalgic smell of school pizza."

Hawthorne pressed a hand to Wren's shoulder, grounding herself for just a breath. It was too quiet. But not the way an empty building was, more like a place holding its breath.

She crept forward, motioning for Andy to follow. They edged toward the swing-door that led into the rest of the school, the one where meal carts must have emerged every day full of lukewarm nuggets and soggy Sloppy Joes.

Hawthorne eased the door open just an inch and heard voices. They weren't panicked or shouting. Instead, she caught a quiet, terse argument in teacher tones. Someone mentioning ration counts. Paper rustling. The unmistakable sound of a child giggling, quickly hushed. She turned back to Andy. "Sounds like they're alive."

Andy's eyes widened, her whole posture unwinding a half-inch from the anxiety coil she'd been carrying. "Let's do this," she said more loudly this time. "I need to find Josh."

"Okay," Hawthorne replied. "Let's go find him without giving the entire sixth grade a heart attack."

They stepped fully into the hallway. Clairemont Middle looked utterly ordinary and completely transformed, a strange liminal space in real time. Posters about Kindness Week and a map of the human body were still taped to the walls. A plastic skeleton stood against the hallway wall, grinning and draped with caution tape someone had playfully looped around its neck. All of it said: normal. Safe. The old world.

And yet, the doors were all closed tight, many marked with taped signs: ROOM FULL. A paper roster taped to a corkboard bore the handwritten addition: "107...students, 26 adults. No one outside after dusk. No exceptions."

Andy's breath hitched quietly as she read it over Hawthorne's shoulder.

"His homeroom is 112."

Hawthorne nodded slowly, heart beating hard against her ribs. "But first we knock, nice and careful."

"Nice and polite!" Wren corrected, and Hawthorne just nodded.

They moved further down the hallway, each door quiet behind its paper signs, until they reached one near the end labeled: Room 112. Andy pointed at it aggressively and then rapped three times. Light. Intentional.

A rustle behind the door, soft voices, then the paper covering the door window was pulled back an inch. A middle-aged woman with half-moon glasses and graying twists peeked through. Her gaze flew to Hawthorne's unfamiliar face, and then to Andy's.

The teacher blinked. "Barista girl?"

Andy gave a sheepish wave. "Yeah. Hi. Sorry I don't have any coffee with me."

A pause. A tightening of the woman's eyes and then, slowly, she pushed the door open.

Inside was soft light from behind the closed vertical blinds over the windows. Desks were clustered into groups. Children blinked at them from desks and art areas, where they were reading and, Hawthorne presumed, doing homework. Near the back, curled into a bean bag with his face in a book was a fragile-looking ten-year-old in a Captain Marvel hoodie.

"Andy?" he said, voice cracking like a hinge.

Time folded in half as Andy darted forward, catching her brother in a full-bodied hug that nearly knocked him off the bean bag. "I got your text, twerp," she murmured against his hair.

"I knew you'd come," he said, arms wrapped tight around her waist.

Hawthorne turned slightly away, wiping at her eyes.

The teacher offered her hand next. "Trisha Lambert," she offered as they shook hands. "You a parent?"

Hawthorne shook her head. "What? No! I'm with her!" She pointed at Andy.

"And I'm with her!" Wren pointed at Hawthorne. "But she's not my daddy."

"Oh! Of course." Trish looked more confused than anything. "We've had a few parents show up, so we've been trying to keep the kids occupied and quiet, but it's complicated with zombies at the door." Her voice was dry but warm in that distinctly teacher-ish way that radiated calm confidence.

"I can imagine," Hawthorne replied, glancing back at the hallway. "We saw a few down by the field fence. They're weirdly quiet out there. Like they're standing guard."

Trisha nodded grimly. "We noticed. They showed up yesterday evening. We were all outside after the storm, waiting for parents, when they all stationed themselves outside the perimeter. A few turned out to be parents themselves, so we had to close the blinds over the windows so the kids wouldn't see." Her brow furrowed. "A few normal parents finally made it here this morning, grabbed their kids and ran out."

Hawthorne nodded slowly, heart breaking for all the kids left waiting for family.

Andy was still kneeling beside Jules, holding on like a second more might make the last thirty hours untangle themselves. Hawthorne let them have it. Instead, she scanned the room again, noting that it seemed prepped for a siege more than anything. She spared a thought to how often active shooter drills had probably made the lockdown easier for the staff.

"Are the other rooms like this?" Hawthorne asked Trisha.

"More or less. The nurse's station has two students with sprained ankles from when the storm hit during recess for squad three. We're lucky with the teachers who survived, and some parents who showed up and decided to stay to help out. At least power is holding." They both looked up at the lights.

"How about food?" Hawthorne asked.

Trisha let out a tired sigh. "We raided the kitchen, but most everything there is ingredients. Mr. Elliott who brought in half a pallet of snack packs late last night from his delivery route when he realized we might be here a while."

Hawthorne blinked. "Wait, which Mr. Elliott?"

"Paul. Drives for QuickSmart Grocery and Catering."

Hawthorne let out a short, stunned breath. "I did ten events with him last year—he always makes an extra stop at the bakery for free pastries when the kids are around. Man's a sweetheart."

"He was a godsend," Trisha agreed, but then frowned. "Haven't heard from him again, though."

Andy stood slowly, Jules tucked up against her. "So now what?"

Hawthorne chewed her lip for a long moment. "Now we don't overstay our welcome."

"Sure, sure," Andy said with obvious disbelief. "How? There are too many people here!"

"Almost one-hundred and fifty." Trisha nodded.

"But also buses, right?" Hawthorne turned to the teacher.

She nodded. "Yes, but no one can agree on where to go. A few parents grabbed their own kids and ran, like I said, but then a couple of the kids wandered back alone and shell shocked. They said they weren't attacked by zombies, just that their parents disappeared. That kept the rest of us in place."

"We've got the agri center at Hayden. It's safe and can sustain a lot of us for a while, until help comes," Hawthorne explained.

Trish's face lit up with relief. "Oh, thank God," Trisha breathed. For the first time, the exhaustion behind her eyes eased, just a fraction. "We've had nothing but patched-up rumors and hope ever since the cell towers got twitchy. The school is a safe space, but we can't hold out for much longer. The kids need real food, as well as a chance to walk around." She gave Hawthorne a look that probably mirrored what some soldiers would give after a tour of war. "They have been *locked inside these rooms for nearly twenty-four hours,*" she said feelingly. "Let's get everyone somewhere safe and we can regroup."

Hawthorne nodded. "We've been calling it the agri center, but honestly? It's the best bet around. We've got greenhouses, trucks, water, first aid, trained adults. It's—" she hesitated, then shrugged, "—not FEMA, but it's something."

"It's more than we've got," Trisha said. "If we can keep the kids calm and quiet through another evening, we can start planning more long-term."

"You'll get help for that," Hawthorne said immediately. "Dr. Mendez is the director of the agri center, and she runs a tight ship."

"That would be great, honestly. We've got our vice-principal but the principal himself went and got himself undead." She shuddered, and leaned in closely, lowering her voice. "Couldn't have happened to a nicer guy," she said sardonically.

"Same for my boss," Hawthorne whispered back. Then she stood up and looked around. "Some of our friends are already en route." She felt her heart swell a little knowing that Leo was on his way and firmly told herself to calm down. They were in the middle of an emergency.

Andy patted her chest like a badge. "Barista recon team reporting for volunteer duty." Her brother rolled his eyes.

"A safe place to go," Trisha mused. "And coffee. You might actually be the cavalry." Her voice cracked a little with dry humor.

Hawthorne turned toward the hallway, her thoughts already spinning. "Once they arrive, we move fast. Get eyes on what's happening outside, get a read of the perimeter, make sure we can keep the zombies distracted while we roll the buses out."

"You think you'll be able to get all of us out?" Trisha asked.

"We're going to try," Hawthorne said. "No 'one van at a time' nonsense. Everyone goes."

Andy nodded and pulled Jules tighter, giving her brother a quick squeeze before guiding him toward one of the classroom corners laid out with granola bars and coloring books. "Guess we're planning a field trip," she said.

Hawthorne exhaled softly. Her plan was half-formed, her fear was simmering, and her legs still itched with nerves. "Trish, can you communicate with the other rooms of survivors? And tell us where to go, maybe. I went to Brekke," she said, looking out the door to the hallway in confusion.

"Sounds good," Trisha said quietly, already reaching for the battered clipboard on the nearby desk. "I'll get an updated headcount from the other rooms." She sighed and shook the pen until it clicked. "You came from Brekke? Then you know the basic layout. They were built around the same time—this wing connects to the cafeteria, which branches out toward the old gym and admin offices. You'll hit your bearings fast."

Hawthorne gave a nod, though her pulse was still jittering like she hadn't unclenched since running into the woods after Wren. "I'll get back to the coffee van to meet the calvary," she said.

"Here's the keys." Andy held up a keyring with a stuffed Koala bear and some anime figurine that Hawthorne did not recognize.

"Thanks." She grabbed the keys and turned to Wren. "Stay here. I'm going out to meet your father and Leo when they get here. I'll need the walkie talkie."

Wren pulled it out of her teddy backpack reluctantly but passed it over without arguing. Hawthorne crouched down. "Hey, no need to get upset. We just need to know you're safe, and you're safe here for now. Be good."

Wren nodded morosely.

"Hi! I'm Ms. Trish. What's your name?" The teacher walked in with experience and efficiency to distract Wren while Hawthorne quickly ducked back into the hallway before the lump rising in her throat had time to announce itself.

The hall stretched ahead, quiet but layered in noise now that she was listening for it. Footsteps, murmurings, the shift of people trying hard not to sound anxious. It felt like an old machine warming up again after months of rust.

She remembered what Leo had told her earlier: No hero moves.

And yet, she didn't feel like she was a movie hero. Nothing she was doing was *heroic.*

But when she glanced back toward Clairemont Middle, with its tired brick and still-bright kid art taped to the locked glass doors, she realized something:

She had found where *her* story turned from merely surviving to sustaining. Her path forward was to unite scared pockets of people into a community working together. Teachers, students, college students, food truck workers, retirees, and whoever else wanted to work with them.

As she locked herself back into the Perky Uppy, she thought that it was time to roll... with food trucks and school buses and hope crafted from caffeine and stubbornness.

She decided this wasn't the end of the world. It was the start of building a new one.

CHAPTER 9

If You Can't Take the Heat

The first truck that rolled into the Clairemont lot was Leo's.

The facilities truck from the agri center pulled around slowly, its dented lime-green fender catching glints of weak sunlight as it rounded the bend into the drive. It looked utterly mundane, just a battered work vehicle with a case of storm-scuff and a stubborn engine, but Hawthorne's whole chest lifted at the sight of it. Relief bloomed, fast and hot and a little embarrassing.

"There they are," she breathed, not realizing she'd been holding her breath.

Just behind him came The Wrap & Roll, rocking over the potholes but unmistakably whole. Its signage was muddy, and one of the side mirrors had clearly seen some action, but it was intact. Daniel was behind the wheel, hunched forward like he was willing it to go faster.

She gave a hard rap to the van horn, but not too loud, just enough to let them know they'd made visual contact. The Perky Uppy let out a cheery little beep, completely inappropriate for a zombie horror movie, and Hawthorne laughed.

Leo's truck came to a stop behind an abandoned school bus, The Wrap & Roll taking the spot beside hers, nose angled inward like it was trying to kiss the curb.

Both of them jumped out at nearly the same time.

"Where is she?" Dan called, far too loud.

"Shhhh! She's inside with the teachers and Andy. Room 112. Kitchen side door is open!"

He was off like a shot before she even finished talking, running around the building to get to his daughter as quickly as possible. Hawthorne smiled, glad that she had been able to give him good news. She turned at the sound of boots on gravel, clicking closer with every step.

Leo.

Just... Leo.

Rough around the edges and calm as ever, face unreadable until she caught his eyes. Buried under the usual careful control was a flicker of raw concern. He didn't say anything at first, but then again, he didn't need to.

She stepped away from the Perky Uppy's door, the sudden stillness between them almost too much to bear. The faint whirr of a distant transformer still fighting for life and a bird calling wildly somewhere behind the school made up the only soundtrack. They stood ten feet apart, both of them slightly dusty, slightly ridiculous, and entirely relieved to be looking at each other in one piece.

"You're okay," Leo said finally, softly, like a reassurance he had to speak into the world to make stick.

She nodded. "You're late."

He huffed a breath, and the side of his mouth kicked up like she'd meant it to be funny. "Detour. Road closed for construction."

She had to laugh at that. Closed road detours in the zombie apocalypse? Of course there were. "You good to go?" she asked, stepping closer, eyes already scanning the parking lot around them.

His smile faltered into something gentler. "Are you?"

"Holding it together with rubber bands and old gum. So, yeah. Miles ahead."

He looked at her for a long second. She was pretty sure half of her face was still smudged with dirt, and definitely sure she had coffee grounds embedded in her clothes, but Leo nodded with the softest smile she had ever seen. Finally, he let the tension slope out of his shoulders. "I'm glad you're okay, Hawthorne."

There was a strange fullness in her chest then, and she shook it off. She had expected Leo to bring up the angry radio exchange, but instead, he said something infinitely worse:

"I knew you'd go."

She paused mid-step.

"I didn't want you to," he continued. "But I knew you would, because I get the feeling you can't leave people behind."

Something tightened in her throat, thin and raw-edged, and she mentally damned him for saying it with kindness. She managed a short, uneven laugh. "And you're not even mad?"

"I was," he admitted. "I thought you had left *me* behind." He glanced away, as if ashamed of himself.

"I—"

"No, let me finish. I was mad, but then you told me to follow, that you wanted me to be a part of your plans. I still wasn't happy," he admitted with a frown. "But here you are, waiting for me."

"How about if I promise not to make it a habit to leave you behind," she said, grabbing his hand instinctively.

He took it and threaded their fingers together as they walked. "I'll hold you to that."

They moved together toward the kitchen entrance as she explained their plans in hushed tones.

"I'll feel better when the kids are on those buses and we're all headed back to the agri center," Hawthorne finished. "Those shufflers just standing around... I don't like it."

"No one does." He opened the door with one last look around them at the zombies standing like broken statues around the perimeter. "They're *too* quiet. That's not random decay slowing them down, that feels more like they are watching us."

"*28 Days Later* did not prepare me for *this*," Hawthorne complained, closing the door behind them and leading Leo into the school's hallways.

"Using the buses is a good idea." He looked around. "And I agree. We need to be technical advisors on any zombie movies from here on out."

They rounded a corner to find a hallway busy with adults and kids sorting themselves out. Andy strode up to them, her brother clinging to her hip and a brass whistle looped around her wrist.

"They're ready," she said. "Mostly. You know, as ready as over one hundred kids, thirty terrified parents, and fifteen teachers hyped up on cold coffee and granola bars can be."

Daniel stepped forward, Wren also tucked close. "I'll be driving one of the buses," he said. "I got my CDL a while ago, not that I think it matters right now." He handed the keys to his truck off to Hawthorne as she passed the van's keys back to Andy. She tossed them in the air once.

"I'm going out and getting the van to pull it around back." She gave a thumbs up to Trish. "Meet you all there!"

Hawthorne nodded sharply. "Get them loaded quietly and steady," she said to Trish and another adult next to her, who both quickly went to start corralling people. She turned to Leo. "You lead in the agri truck, and I'll take The Wrap & Roll out last. Bring up the rear."

He nodded once, purposeful calm already settling into place like his well-worn tool belt. "We'll be fine."

And for a moment, Hawthorne believed him.

Until a group of kids outside Room 108 burst into noise.

It wasn't loud at first, just a gasp, the startled sob of a child, and then, the rising cacophony of small voices in confused terror. Hawthorne spun instinctively toward it, nearly colliding with Andy, who had surged forward with Jules clutched to her side.

"No, no, no!" someone was whispering over and over again, and then a clearer scream pushed its way out through the hallway: "That's my mom! That's MY MOM!"

Hawthorne's stomach dropped.

Out the windows lining that section of the hallway, one of the zombies had wandered closer to the building, crossing some invisible boundary, eyes locked on the children gathered behind the glass.

Another scream joined it. A small boy yelling "Daddy!" in a voice that scraped like it had been pulled from the hinge of grief.

Daniel tensed beside her.

The air inside the school shifted, as if the collective panic of just a few voices cracked the seal on something much larger, deeper, and colder...something that had been teetering on the edge of chaos and just got pushed over.

A low, grinding growl echoed from outside. Not loud, but close. Close enough that even the weariest kids now froze like prey animals, sensing the forest going wrong.

"We need to move," Leo murmured beside her, no longer calm but steeled. Prepared.

Trisha bolted into the hallway from one of the rooms. Her face was pale beneath her deep brown skin. "Are they moving in? Are we under attack?"

One of the teachers, a twitchy older man with thinning hair and trembling hands, shoved past them, eyes wild. "I can't do this again," he yelled. "I can't—I saw what happened to Mr. Brewer yesterday! It's everyone for themselves!"

"No! Wait!" Trisha grabbed for him, but he broke free.

He ran straight down the main hallway, slamming against a door that faced the schoolyard and forcing it open. Through the now-open door, Hawthorne could see that two zombies had already crept forward. They turned at the sound of his furious yelling, then surged. He let out a single shriek as they grabbed him just as the doors slammed shut, and it echoed through the halls.

Children screamed. One of the fire extinguishers clattered to the floor as someone dropped it from where they pulled it off the wall.

"They weren't attacking before," Hawthorne said hoarsely as several adults tried to calm down the kids.

"They aren't after the kids," Leo said, eyes hard. "They are basically easy prey, but they aren't even trying to get in. Everything was quiet until the kids screamed and that teacher blew the lid off everything."

Hawthorne's mind raced with the sudden insight that hit her, pulling together all the threads of the past thirty-six hours. It was all about negative emotions. Anger, fear, panic... That's what drew them.

"I think they respond to negative emotions," she said, stepping back as Andy herded Jules around her, running for her van in the front parking lot. Hawthorne faced off with Leo. "Fight me!"

"What?" He looked at her as if she had lost her mind. She thought maybe she had, because it was a long shot, but more kids were screaming in fear, and more zombies were crawling over the school fencing.

Hawthorne turned to Trish. "We'll lead them away to give you all time to get the buses loaded." Trish and Andy did not even question it, moving quickly to get the survivors moving toward the back of the school where the buses were lined up.

She turned to Leo again. "Fight me!"

"*What?*" Leo repeated in confusion.

"Fight me, you pretentious asshole!" Hawthorne pulled on every furious, terrified thought that had crossed her mind in the last twenty-four hours, pointed her finger dead in Leo's face, and bellowed. "The zombies are fucking attracted to outbursts of negative emotions, so *we're gonna fight about it!* Who the fuck are you to tell me what I can and can't do?"

He stepped backwards and blinked in shock for a moment before the penny dropped. "Excuse me for giving a damn about you!" He shouted back. They started moving toward the front of the school, where Dan had left The Wrap & Roll truck. "Maybe I just don't want to have to go running off after a suicidal idiot!"

It didn't feel *real* enough, though. She needed true, red-hot anger. Shaking her head, she glanced over at Leo. "I can't keep being mad at you! I'm going to pretend you're Frank!"

He nodded. "Good idea! You're my first thesis adviser." He grimaced as he said it, clearly reviving bad memories.

The zombies were moving slowly but drawn inexorably toward the noise, the fear, the emotional electricity churning the air around the school. Their forms emerged from behind crumbling hedgerows and idle swing sets one by one, like a dreadful procession summoned by some invisible horn, and from the windows Hawthorne could tell they were aiming for her and Leo, not the back parking lot and the buses.

Hawthorne started jogging while she screamed at Leo about Frank and her shitty job and all her bad luck.

"Frank!" she shouted at the schoolyard sky as she slammed the front doors open, voice cracking like a whip through the rising cacophony. "You smug, trust fund parasite! You paid fifty thousand dollars for a food truck and still managed to ruin every minimum wage employee's life inside six months!"

Leo jogged beside her, breath short and sharp. "You told five people to defrost chicken in the sun, Frank!"

"Oh my god, you remember that? That was only my second day on the job!"

"It haunts me!" Leo roared, voice raw with something both furious and gleeful. He whirled, planting his feet and shouting toward the playground fence. "And you—Dr. Overton! You smug dinosaur in a tweed coat! Just because you got your PhD during the Cold War doesn't mean it's still 1982! You talked down to every female student like their ovaries disqualified their research!"

A zombie at the far end of the monkey bars stuttered to a stop and turned, joining the slow tide of undead heading for them.

Hawthorne half-laughed, half-hissed, "Get personal! It's working!" She saw the truck, but it was too soon, the rest of the survivors needed time to clear the school grounds entirely. She veered right and Leo followed as she made a slow, zig-zag trek across the parking lot.

Leo's eyes sparked. "You told me I was 'better off in the administrative track' because I 'wasn't creative enough for real research!' Well, guess what, you self-centered prick? I'm already on tenure track and I'm not even forty! Suck that!"

"We're out here saving children, Frank, while you rot in pieces! That's all your worthless ass is good for!" Hawthorne shouted behind them. "You may have written me up for being 'insubordinate,' but at least I never cried in the cab because your trophy girlfriend called you a fast-food worker!"

The zombies were moving toward them now. Still slow by living-human standards, but their sluggishness had purpose.

"That's right! Come on!" Hawthorne bellowed, hopping back and forth like she was trying out for the world's worst boxing competition. "I NEVER CALLED IN SICK, FRANK. I HAD STREP AND YOU SAID MY 'VIBES WERE OFF'!"

Leo's shout cracked beside her. "ALSO, DR. OVERTON—YOUR 'DISRUPTIVE TECHNIQUES' COURSE WAS JUST TWENTY DIFFERENT WAYS TO STROKE YOUR EGO!"

They swerved left behind a line of parked cars, drawing an increasing ripple of groaning corpses in their wake. The zombies were unmistakably following them, heads tilted, limbs dragging, eyes vacant but locked onto the chaos like a dog scenting meat.

Each scream, each shouted insult, drew more of them out from the trees, from behind dumpsters, from where they'd been waiting in that preternatural stillness. They didn't run and they didn't sprint, they lurch-stepped like drunks during spring break.

Hawthorne almost tripped on a loose curb, caught herself before face planting. "You ever tell off that Overton?" she yelled breathlessly.

Leo leaned beside her and gasped, "No, but this is the best catharsis I've had since I took boxing classes."

"Better than boxing," she croaked. "Now you're screaming at the gaping maw of the undead. Real career growth."

"Therapeutic, educational. Honestly?" He looked behind them and winced. "Effective."

The moaning chorus behind them was picking up volume as more zombies entered the lot. None of them even so much as glanced toward the school building anymore. Fear-muffled sobs still echoed faintly from around the back of the school, but with Hawthorne and Leo throwing psychological landmines like confetti, the zombies followed the emotions giving them the most bang for the buck.

The nasty things Hawthorne usually kept buried apparently made the best bait, she realized.

Hawthorne took a deep breath and roared, face turned upward: "TO THE LADY WHO SAID I WASN'T 'FOOD TRUCK PRETTY'—YOUR LASH EXTENSIONS LOOKED LIKE A TIM BURTON NIGHTMARE!"

More zombies approached the school in shambling unison, no longer indifferent bystanders. They were drawn like moths to fire, slouching inexorably toward the couple shouting their infuriated grievances at the world.

"THE DUDE WHO SAID I'D BE PRETTIER IF I SMILED—" Hawthorne shouted, banging on the hood of a sedan, "I HOPE YOU GOT STUCK AT AIRPORT SECURITY AND LOST YOUR WALLET!"

Leo swiveled on one foot, waving his arms wide like a deranged carnival barker. "AND TO THE PROFESSOR WHO TOLD ME I 'LACKED PASSION' AND THEN STOLE MY RESEARCH FOR HIS PAPER—MAY YOU BE HAUNTED BY THE A.L.A. STYLE MANUAL!"

Each verbal slap to a ghost of their past carved a clear path as zombies turned en masse, each shriek and growl echoing their route. Their groans knit together into a dull siren of horror, trailing Hawthorne and Leo like sluggish, rotting ducklings.

Behind them, unseen but welcome noise, the bus engines sputtered to life.

Hawthorne just barely heard Trisha's voice barking logistics over the din of zombies. "Cluster A, you're with Daniel! Cluster D with me! No pushing, inside like we practiced!" And Andy, somewhere close, shouted, "Parents who stick to the plan get a free latte!"

"I think it's working, sounds like they are heading out," Leo muttered.

"Unless they're suddenly here for dinner theater instead, I'm gonna give it a solid 'yes,'" Hawthorne hissed, swinging around the side of a truck and luring the horde further into the parking lot.

Bus doors slammed shut, one after the next.

Engines coughed. Then growled. Then roared.

Hawthorne let silence stretch in her chest for a heartbeat as the sound of tires turning on asphalt cut through everything else. The buses rolled out from the back, picking up speed as they steered off the school grounds, all four buses humming with precious cargo. Dan, Trisha, and a couple of other teachers were each driving.

The Van That Could—Perky Uppy—rattled at the rear under Andy's impassioned navigation, one hand on the wheel steering while the other handed a juice box to her brother. She gave Hawthorne a distracted thumbs up as they roared past.

They were moving, and they were safe.

Hawthorne grabbed Leo's hand. "To the truck! Now!" They broke out in a run around the back of the truck. The zombies already focused on them started closing in.

Leo yanked open the door and Hawthorne dove past him into the driver's seat.

"Close the door! Close it!" She fumbled the keys out of her jacket pocket and jammed them into the ignition with trembling hands, praying the stupid truck didn't stall.

"On it!" Leo yanked it shut a second later, one undead hand slapping wetly against the glass before he flipped the latch to lock it. "*Go!*"

She didn't need to be told twice. Foot on the gas, hands sweaty-slick on the wheel, she threw it into drive and peeled away from the curb with a squeal of rubber.

The horde lunged too late, a few bodies staggering after them in a grotesque mockery of a sprint. Most drifted forward with hollow groans, still caught in the emotional wake they'd carved through the lot, the humming haze of fury, shame, and old wounds made manifest.

The food truck bounced hard over a post-storm pothole and Hawthorne fought to keep her grip steady. The smell of old cumin and steam-seasoned vinyl filled the cabin, a memory from before the world tipped sideways.

"Are they following?" she asked, not daring to glance in the mirrors.

Leo twisted to look backwards out the side window, breath ragged. "Slower now. Some still moving, but I think the bonfire we gave them is going cold. They aren't sprinters, anyway," he added with obvious relief.

They hit the edge of the school block, clear of the worst of it. The road ahead stretched wide and nearly empty of stalled cars, and for a few minutes, the only sound was the high whine of the engine and Hawthorne's heavy breathing.

She didn't realize her foot was still pressed nearly to the floor until Leo reached over and gently touched the back of her hand.

"Hawthorne."

She didn't answer. Couldn't. The tremble started in her spine and radiated outward in bone-deep waves. Her grip on the wheel went white-knuckle tight and stayed there, even as the speed dropped below thirty, even as they left the worst of it behind.

"Hawthorne," Leo said again, softer this time. "You don't have to keep holding everything together. The kids are headed to the agri center. You did it."

She blinked and tried to focus, but everything was frayed, like her insides had been scraped clean and she was just waiting for the rest to fall through.

"I can't stop," she whispered, voice cracking under its own weight. "If I stop, if I breathe, it all floods in—the dead teachers, the kids screaming, Frank's smug face!" Her laugh came out wrong and hollow. "The way they looked at us. We were bait, Leo. I lured people-shaped monsters like I was leading a goddamn birthday parade. I screamed myself hoarse... and it worked." As she talked, she let up on the gas until they rolled to a stop.

Leo didn't flinch. He just reached over again, not for her hand this time, but to turn the ignition off. The truck sighed into silence, cabin going still except for their shallow breaths and the faint tick of cooling metal.

Wind brushed the windows, bringing the smell of wet asphalt and far-off wildflowers, the kind of scent that she thought shouldn't belong anymore, and yet somehow, it tethered her.

"Look at me," he said.

She turned.

No pretense in his expression now. Just open concern, gentle but fierce. He spoke low, like every word was steadied with intention. "You didn't lead monsters," he said. "You drew them away so kids could live. You used your valid anger like a lure to keep other people safe. And yeah, it's awful and strange and shouldn't have worked, but it did because *you* knew what they'd hear. You figured it out, while the rest of us just sat around panicking."

Her lip trembled. "It still doesn't feel like enough. I'm still shaking like I'm gonna fall apart."

"Then fall," he said, simply. "I've got you."

She folded forward, covering her face with both hands. A sound slipped out, half sob, half laugh, and all exhaustion. Leo pulled her toward him as he stood next to the driver's seat, arms circling her shoulders as if it was the most natural thing for him to do in the broken world around them.

She leaned into him like a wave giving up the shore, buried her face in his chest until the heartbeat under his flannel shirt anchored her more than the seatbelt she hadn't remembered to put on.

"I hate Frank so much," she mumbled into Leo's collarbone.

"I hate Dr. Overton's beard," he replied.

That cracked her into a laugh-sob that splintered the last bit of frozen courage she'd been holding tight. She didn't move for a long, precarious minute, tucked into him like he was home as she cried.

Leo shifted just enough to press a slow kiss into Hawthorne's temple, his fingers brushing a leaf from the tangled edge of her ponytail. When she didn't pull away, when she stayed there breathing against him like the whole world had finally exhaled, he tilted his head down. Their foreheads touched first.

Then, so softly it felt like a breath catching instead of a choice, he kissed her.

It was quiet and warm and unexpected in its gentleness. No urgency. Just the shape of something long overdue finally falling into place, slotted like spoons in a drawer.

Hawthorne had been kissed a lot of ways in her life—in alleys behind restaurants, on tables sticky with old grease, awkwardly during movie nights that smelled like popcorn and teenage hormones.

But never like this.

Never like someone was asking her to stay.

She kissed him back, slow and certain, one hand fisting lightly in the front of his flannel shirt. The world didn't fall away. It stayed, tireless and complicated and cracked, but just for that second, it tilted a little more gently.

And then—

Knock-knock-knock.

The sound was sharp but not frantic, three quick raps on the stainless steel frame beneath the driver-side window. Not a drag or thump like undead fingers. Just polite, practice-knock human rhythm.

They froze, lips still brushing. Hovering.

"Was that… real?" Leo whispered.

Hawthorne blinked. "The kiss or the knock?"

A pause.

"Yes," he said.

She smiled, heart still rattling in her chest. "Very real. Both."

Another knock. "Hello? Hello!" A woman's voice called out. "Are you human in there?

Hawthorne frowned at how normal she sounded. "Yes?"

Leo bit down on a laugh.

"Oh good! Can I get a bar-b-qued pork wrap?"

Leo stepped forward cautiously and unlatched the door to slide it open.

Outside stood a woman in her late thirties, curly hair tied back with what looked like a torn glittery scarf, wearing a windbreaker and jeans streaked with ash and dried mud. Beside her, a teenaged boy hunched like he'd rather be invisible but was still trying to play it cool, hands jammed deep into the pockets of an oversized hoodie that read "Lincoln Falcons Track & Field."

"Sorry to bother y'all," she called again, her Southern accent rounding the edges of every word like a warm biscuit. "We saw the truck roll up and wanted to make sure you weren't... you know, brain-munchers."

Leo blinked. "We're officially not."

"Great," she said brightly. "Because The Wrap & Roll is one of my favorite food trucks in town and I swear to Jesus if there's any pulled pork left in this county, I will trade you a dozen C batteries and a gallon of sweet tea."

Behind her, the teenager groaned, mortified. "Mom!"

"I'm not ashamed, Dylan!"

Leo ran a hand down his face. "You're joking, right?"

"Sounds like a deal to me," Hawthorne said with a shrug as she followed Leo out onto the cracked pavement.

The woman squinted at her. "Chef Porter?"

Hawthorne blinked. "Wait, what?"

"You catered my niece's graduation party last May. You made hush-puppies that made my ex mother-in-law cry."

The boy nodded with a sharp grin. "We got pix."

Hawthorne gave the mother-son duo a once-over scan. They wore exhaustion and the kind of emotional unraveling that came from trying to hold things together after thirty-plus straight hours of societal collapse.

"I don't know what's in the inventory," Hawthorne said, stepping back into the truck, stopping to open up the side order window. "But if there's pork and it hasn't spoiled, you're getting lunch."

Blessedly, The Wrap & Roll's fridge was still running off the backup battery. She found a sealed bag of sweet smoked shredded pork in the cold bin, some cabbage slaw that had only wilted a bit, and several stacks of Dan's trademark homemade tortillas. "We're a go!"

Glancing at the sky—still mercifully overcast but not threatening—she decided it was fate. She fired up the griddle.

The smell hit the air within seconds, a warm, spicy, tangy smokey scent curling out through the open order window like a lighthouse signal. Across the cracked street, a curtain twitched. Five minutes later, a man in pajama pants and hiking boots wandered out of a side yard with a wary look and a shotgun slung over his arm. "Am I smelling real food?" he croaked.

"Depends," the woman called back over her shoulder. "Can you say 'please,' Chaz?"

He rolled his eyes as he walked up, clearly familiar with his neighbor's personality.

"Plate up!" Hawthorne said, plating the first wrap with a flourish and a dollop of slaw. Dylan tried to give it to his mother, but she waved a hand at him, and he wolfed it down.

The neighbor's eyes widened, and he raised a hand as if in supplication. "Oh, my God, I'll say it in fifteen languages. My last meal was two string cheese sticks and a stress cry."

"I accept your currency," Hawthorne replied, flipping another tortilla. "Form a line. I've got enough fuel for maybe a dozen, depending on who gets feisty with the sauces. Leo, you're up for plating." She pointed. "There are the paper baskets. There is the slaw." He quickly got to work.

The mom—Darla, as she introduced herself—accepted the second wrap reverently. Her son took his with a thank-you-and-a-grunt combo so classically teenager it felt like the universe was finding its balance again.

A few more people emerged from the neighborhood's edges in ones and twos, drawn by the scent and the sound of people gathering. There was no panic, and no rush, just cautious hope wearing beat-up shoes and windbreakers.

"Is this what I think it is?" one middle-aged woman asked as she accepted a steaming, folded wrap with slaw.

"If you think it's southern healing in a tortilla, then yeah," Hawthorne said, grinning for the first time in what felt like hours.

"She's not wrong," muttered a man with a missing sneaker and two duct-taped wrist splints.

Once the small crowd was fed, someone off to the side asked the question that was clear on all of their faces: "Where do we go now? What do we do?"

Hawthorne didn't hesitate. "There's a survivor's base at the Hayden agri center on campus," she told them, handing out a tea cup to a woman holding a cat in a sling carrier. "We've got resources and some decent people."

"Can't fit the whole city in there," Chaz mumbled, licking his fingers. "Also, it's all the way out on the edge of town.

Hawthorne nodded regretfully, Leo mirroring her, although she was secretly amused because only in Fairhope could a university campus seven miles from downtown be considered "all the way out on the edge of town."

"No, but we've got supplies and three food trucks. We'll come back," Hawthorne said, voice clear now, strong even through the weariness swelling in her chest. "We'll set up again tomorrow at the old buffet—main road's clear just north of here." She knew they knew the place. It was big, familiar, and ridiculous. If people saw life there, they'd come.

"The place with the defaced sign?" Darla asked, chomping the last bite of her wrap. "Says 'End Times' in bright red paint?"

Hawthorne grinned. "That's the one. Looked like a joke last week. Looks like a prophecy now."

A round of chuckles rippled through the ragtag group, the kind of laughter that doesn't come easy after a trauma, but clings to hope.

Leo leaned out from the truck window, wiping his hands on a dishtowel. "We'll be back with more food, updated info, and probably a whiteboard for sign-ins. Spread the word if you know where people are holed up."

A murmur of understanding passed through the little cluster of neighbors. Some nodded. Others seemed to tuck the information into tired eyes. A teenage girl bit into her wrap while holding her grandmother's hand. Darla pulled an old receipt from her purse and scribbled "TUES - BUFFET - FOOD" on the back with a half-dead pen.

"I'll tell everyone who still remembers what hot food tastes like," she said.

"And bring those C batteries," Leo added with a smirk. "For trade."

"We run a high-class operation," Hawthorne mock-whispered.

Leo looked at her, and for a long second, it was just them again.

Side-by-side at a food truck window in the apocalypse, making magic happen for ordinary people.

It wasn't much but it was a start. And tomorrow?

Tomorrow, she'd start cooking again.

CHAPTER 10
Epilogue

The central kitchen of the agri center thrummed with low, purposeful energy. It did not feel rushed or chaotic like so many kitchens Hawthorne had worked in over the years, but instead it had a warm, focused noise usually reserved for Saturday morning brunches back in her parent's home. She wondered how it was holding up. They had made a trip back there a few days ago that was essentially a "smash and grab" but it got her fresh clothes and her mother's collection of rare succulent plants that Carlos was still cooing over.

Six days into the apocalypse and Mendez had overseen about ten such missions, which picked up both personal belongings and, sometimes, stranded family members to bring back to the center. Eli had led several missions to local schools and nursing homes, but many people they came across were already setting up community centers for mutual aid, though, so there wasn't the expectation that there would be many more additions to the agri center. In fact, at least thirty of the kids they had rescued from Clairemont had ended up going home to their remaining family members, which lessened the load on the agri center's infrastructure, to Leo's great relief since he had taken over as de facto "head of facilities."

Trisha had been crowned principal of the ad hoc school/orphanage, and roped Shelly into helping her and the other teachers get it organized over in the James H. Washington Community Center, which had plenty of large rooms and auditorium-style classrooms. Hawthorne and Daniel were in the middle of making lunch for them, featuring huge trays of vegetarian casseroles with noodles "sourced" from one of the grocery stores near campus.

The communications systems had gone down completely on day three, and there was no indication that the National Guard or the Army or anyone was coming anytime soon. No one had even seen any planes in the air since before the super storm had hit Fairhope.

As for the zombies...they were still there, watching. Sometimes they were spotted fighting each other, and every once in a while, they would converge somewhere to attack people. Hawthorne had shared her theory about that with Mendez, so she knew the de facto leader of their commune (for lack of a better word) was living up to her scientific training by tracking the incidents they found out about with a map and charts and probably spreadsheets. Sounded like homework to her.

Less talked about were the "ghosts" that appeared to people every once in a while. Those were more easily dismissed, but every time, Leo would give her a piercing look, obviously remembering what she had told him about the woman she saw during The Wrap & Roll rescue operation. Hawthorne had theories about them, too, but kept them to herself. Daniel assumed that Wren seeing Adrien's "ghost" meant his husband was dead, and for the moment Hawthorne did not have any evidence to the contrary. But the way the woman had looked at her was burned into her mind, and nothing about that incident made her think "soul of the dead." She wasn't sure what it *did* make her think of, though, so for the moment it was a mystery no one could solve.

Hawthorne wiped off her palm with her apron as she leaned over the map spread across the prep table. It looked tragic, having been printed on campus printer paper, had coffee spilled on it at some point, and was covered in hastily scribbled notes like "avoid car pileup," "Bucket's by gas station," and "Carlos's weird detour with the goats???"

"So," Hawthorne said, tapping just below the words 'Darla's neighborhood.' "We clear the route up Elliot Road, swing past the twin gas stations—"

"And end up at French Line park," Rucha finished, flipping a page in her rapidly filling clipboard. "Yesterday, we got four people to show up there, so I say we hang there for at least an hour to see who else might creep out of the woodwork. Then we head out, and even if Reyes corner still has shufflers, we can loop through Morrow Street and hit End Times Buffet by noon."

Dan scratched his chin, his daughter's rainbow hair barrettes still clipped to his wrist like a bracelet. "We're down to two full propane tanks for the day, so the Wrap'll need to stick with grilled cheese, vegan chili, maybe muffins. Keep the meat use minimal."

Dr. Mendez strode into the kitchen with unshakable purpose and the unmistakable whiff of damp corduroy, clipboard in one hand, thermos in the other. Her dark green flannel shirt sleeves were rolled halfway up her forearms, revealing a series of minor scratches, and there was what looked suspiciously like a hickey on her neck. Marla walked in right behind Mendez, radiating lavender and smug satisfaction.

Hawthorne groaned theatrically. "For the love of carbs, can we flirt after the logistics meeting, please?"

"Why wait?" her mother asked as she set a bundle of solar-charged mason jar lanterns and a turmeric lemon juice in a banged-up water bottle on the counter. "Raiding for supplies is deeply sensual work."

Mendez didn't miss a beat. "Especially when co-led by a woman who can match citrus notes with danger."

Rucha snorted. "Oh, my god. You two are insufferable."

"And yet," Dan muttered to no one in particular, "I'm rooting for them. It's like watching a slow-burn fanfic unfold in real life."

Mendez flashed a rare, teasing smile then got down to business. "Grid's starting to blink out again outside the core. Kiss your precious refrigeration goodbye if we don't start pulling perishables now. I want to put together a run to clean out the big-box stores—just the perishables first run, frozen stuff and eggs, whatever protein we can salvage."

"We've got new wheels for the job," Rucha added, clicking her pen at the ready and pointing meaningfully at Eli, who stood off to the side, watching everyone in his stoic way. Hawthorne sometimes forgot he was there. "Eli and I 'secured' four grocery delivery vans. All hybrids, decent range on battery alone. Might need minor repairs, but Eli says he can trick at least two into functioning at full speed."

Andy appeared from the next room like a cape-less espresso superhero, balancing a tray of mugs. "You know what else is fully functioning?" she said with a grin. "My new espresso bar! Enjoy your caffeine courtesy of the newly christened Cozy Cauldron, Home of Ascended Latte Machines and Post-Apocalyptic Hospitality."

She set the tray down to a collection of wary looks. Her bright pastel blue puffy jacket covered in cute animal patches was way too clean to reflect the chaos of the week, and she wore it like a statement of kawaii superiority. "Who wants foam art?" she sang.

"That's a crime," Dan murmured, staring at his cup with a mixture of awe and horror.

"It's cute," Hawthorne said mildly, accepting a cappuccino crowned with a mediocre foam cat and giving it a sip. "Also, where did you even find that?"

Andy grinned. "It's magic!"

"She stole the espresso machine from the college library's coffee closet," Eli said drily.

"Liberated!" Andy replied acidly, glaring at him.

"Liberated, right. Like I liberated three gallons of half-melted butter from that pizza shop yesterday," Eli said, arms folded across his chest while he sipped his black coffee like it doubled as demon repellent.

Hawthorne raised her cup to him. "Bless you for your dairy crimes. Some of that butter went straight into the cornbread last night."

Maggie nodded solemnly. "Tasted like hope and heaven." She had attached herself to the kitchen team, and several of the newer members of the agri center were her family, including her incredibly old grandmother who talked with a Jamaican accent so thick only Maggie and Med-Student Jake could understand her.

Marla leaned against the counter with the easy grace of someone who had once hitchhiked through six national parks without a map when she was in her thirties. "Let me know when you're ready for a homebrew kombucha raid," she said to Mendez with a wink. "Got a contact over near Larkspur with a fridge still running. If the grid holds up through the weekend, we might score at least half his SCOBYs."

"I love it when you talk microbial," Mendez said, deadpan but clearly delighted.

Rucha half-choked on her coffee. "I am this close to instituting a PDA tax."

"You'd be rich," Andy muttered, slurping the foam off a tiny demitasse cup, ignoring the pained looks Eli kept sending her way.

As the laughter finally started to settle down, footsteps scuffed at the side entrance and Hawthorne looked up instinctively, already knowing who it was before he even finished swinging the door shut behind him.

Leo.

He looked travel-worn and wind-rumpled, khakis streaked with dust and a clipboard tucked under one arm, but his face lit up the second he saw her. Not in some sweeping, rom-com flourish, but far more subtle. Real. Like just seeing her let him take the first full breath in hours.

"You made it back," she said, not even realizing she was walking toward him until she was already lifting her arms.

"I always will," he said, pulling her in without hesitation.

His arms wrapped around her middle, her apron still peppered with bits of diced vegetables. She tucked her face against his ubiquitous flannel shirt, inhaling the warm, slightly musty scent of someone who'd lifted too many produce crates before breakfast.

Behind them, someone muttered, "They're just as bad," followed by Dan's saucy whistle and Rucha stage-whispering, "We're all watching, but we're pretending not to."

"You are not being subtle," Leo said over her shoulder.

"I'm not being paid to be subtle," Rucha called back, flipping a clipboard page like a mic drop.

"You're not being paid," Dr. Mendez said with a sigh and an unsubtle eye-roll.

Hawthorne let the laughter and warmth wash over her like a balm, the kind she never would've admitted she'd needed. The apocalypse was supposed to end things—lives, structures, the illusion of order. But all it really did was crack things open and show what was still worth saving. Now, the survivors were making space for what could grow in the wreckage.

And weirdly enough, what was growing the strongest looked a lot like hope. Fermented and foraged, sure. Run on solar panels, adrenaline, and hot coffee, yes. But real.

She stepped back from Leo just a bit, enough to see the soft crinkle near the corner of his eyes, the scruff collecting along his jaw. This man had shown her how to siphon gas with a cut hose and a bucket the day before, and it had been the most romantic date she ever had in her life.

"I saved you a breakfast bar," she said softly, and handed him a paper-wrapped something she had slapped together with oats, dried blueberries, and optimism in the form of 'liberated' peanut butter.

"You spoil me," he said with a crooked smile.

A sudden clatter near the sink snapped her attention back to the crowded kitchen. Carlos had been trying to load four mismatched colanders into a single drawer and dropped all of them. Rucha was laughing as she picked them up while he blushed furiously and Maggie made fun of them. When Hawthorne had first walked into this kitchen, the place echoed. Now it spoke constantly: a creaky drawer here, someone shouting across the prepping tables, the gurgle of an old-fashioned water kettle.

"We were just going over staging for the next Buffet run tomorrow," Hawthorne said, looping her arm through Leo's and steering him toward the map again. "We've got two new food trucks brought in from the east loop, plus Andy's Perky Uppy."

"Including Renzo's InkaTruck!" Rucha clapped happily. "He's even alive to run it!"

"Oh, I love Peruvian food," Marla sighed happily.

"*Anyway*, I want to do a regular run going by the south side, stop at French Line Park and then end up at the End Times Country Buffet. Give it some real base-camp energy."

"That's its official name now?" Mendez asked, one arm slung over Marla's shoulders.

"As official as it gets!" Hawthorne said with a smile.

Leo raised a brow. "Official and permanent?"

"As permanent as anything can be a week into the zombie apocalypse, yeah." She spread her fingers across the map, anchoring it with flattened hands. "It's central, shaded most of the day, close enough to safe zones that people will be willing to walk it. If we make it feel like a given, like a place people are expected to pass through on the regular, it'll be easier for more of them to show up. Not just the drifters and lucky ones."

"You looking to stage intake?" Carlos asked, now balancing a crate of dented canned goods, some of which were perilously close to falling over.

"I'm looking to stage hope," Hawthorne replied with a soft smile. She had not felt that kind of overarching hope in a while, since probably before her father died five years ago. It felt good.

"I've approved the project," Mendez added. "We're out here on the fringe of the city, on the west side of campus. We're a logical organizational point because of our resources, but we're not centralized," Mendez continued, gesturing with her thermos like a pointer. "Everyone knows 'the old buffet,' so if you tell them to meet us there, they won't go to the wrong place. From there, we can organize delivery networks, stage pickups, and start tracking what areas still have survivors. If we keep the system light—solar-powered where we can, hybrid routes for longer distances—we've got a shot at stabilizing most of the north half of the city. Maybe more."

She leaned against the counter, the weight of leadership heavy but settled, like she'd made peace with it. Hawthorne tried to block out the way her mother give Mendez dopey cow eyes.

"But the agri center taps out at four hundred, maybe four-fifty if we start turning some classrooms into barracks, which is not ideal," Mendez said. "Our infrastructure here won't go far, and we're already pushing it. Some people might eventually leave. In fact, I'm counting on it, but I think a stable population of three hundred can hold for a while. That means we need overflow spaces, satellite zones like the Buffet, where we can triage, coordinate, and rotate crews without overloading any one spot. We can work the larger grocery stores into the system once we're fully established." She paused. "At least until help comes."

There was silence at that, since it was looking less likely by the day that help would come at all.

Hawthorne nodded, tracing her finger in a slow loop around the rough X they'd marked for the End Times Country Buffet on the map. It looked ridiculous but it also looked like the beginning of something important.

Eli shifted from where he stood near the shelves, arms crossed, brow furrowed in his usual deep-thought stance. "We can retrofit two of the new delivery vans as mobile comm hubs," he offered. "If we can scavenge enough relays, we might be able to bootstrap a wireless mesh net between the Buffet and the agri center. Short-range at first, but better than shouting over rooftops."

Andy perked up. "Can I name the network?"

"No," several people said at once.

Hawthorne grinned. They were building something vital and necessary for Fairhope as a whole, and yeah, it looked like reclaimed food trucks and scavenged bins, but in a way, it felt more building back better.

Leo was watching her again, quietly as always, like she was more than the sum of her plans and stress-induced cooking experiments with packaged ramen. He hadn't said much since walking in, but his presence was anchoring and steady, like he could feel the future she was starting to believe in, without needing to poke holes in it.

"You're good at this," he said softly, nudging her shoulder.

"Meh," she replied, huffing a little laugh. "I'm a food truck cook. It makes me good at juggling chaos and cabbage."

"And yet here you are, setting up trade routes and infrastructure while making breakfast bars from scratch," he said, eyes warm with something that made her feel loved.

She looked down at the battered old map, her hands resting at its corners like it was a page from some myth they were still writing. Stubborn pragmatism had gotten her this far, but what came next? Another meeting about logistics? A supply run into the bones of suburbia? Convincing another pocket of survivors that this wasn't just a pit stop but the beginning of something stronger?

Yes. All of it.

"I don't know what I'm doing half the time," she whispered, almost confessing it to the sunbeam slanting in through the dusty window that made the lone strands of silver in Leo's hair sparkle. "But I do know we're not going back. Not really, not the way a lot of people expect us to, and I don't want to rebuild the old mess, honestly. I want to grow something better."

Leo glanced toward the window too, as if trying to see what she saw. "Then let's grow it together."

She nodded once, tight and certain. "Start composting old systems. Use what we can. Shed the rest."

A beat of silence, then Andy piped up cheerfully from the espresso corner, "That was the most romantic punk-rock thing anyone has said all week."

"Or the most agro-hippie," Carlos muttered, setting down the crate with a final thud. "Hard to tell anymore."

"Solar punk?" Mendez asked no one in particular, hand flipping in an either-or motion.

"Yes," Hawthorne said, straightening fully now. Her shoulders didn't feel so heavy anymore—maybe just sore, the way a good hike leaves you. "That's the whole point. Grow gardens out of parking lots and power a revolution with the steam from an ancient espresso machine."

Andy gave a fist-pump too vigorous for her adult-sized sippy cup, which immediately toppled over and rolled dramatically to the edge of the counter. Everyone winced as it went over. Eli caught it one-handed before it hit the tile floor.

"Damn," Rucha said with grudging admiration. "Did you do martial arts or something?"

"I didn't," Eli replied. "I'm just tired of cleaning up Andy's disasters."

Andy shrugged and took the cup from him like nothing had happened. "Keep hating. I'll be over here frothing milk with higher purpose."

As the jokes rippled through the room again, Hawthorne glanced around the room at Marla arguing with Mendez over the merits of fermentation (they seemed to agree, she thought, but were enjoying arguing anyway); Andy brandishing a milk wand like a light saber at Wren, who squealed and fought back with a silicone whisk; Dan trying to explain his tortilla recipe to Carlos who clearly didn't get it; Rucha sketching logistics in a salvaged college notebook; and Eli sitting down with a small box of tools to quietly fix a coffee grinder that Hawthorne had not seen before.

She let herself bask in the moment as Leo wrapped his arms around her from behind and pulled her close. Despite all the chaos of the past few days, she thought it ironically felt like home. Built, not inherited. Her mother was alive and weird and radiant, her new partner steady as the ground beneath her heavy boots. They were all her people now, and if it was a family born out of tragedy and terror, that did not change what they had become.

If they had to build a new world out of scavenged appliances, greenhouses, old flower planters, and solar-charged stubbornness, then Hawthorne figured they were already halfway there.

Want more?

Love the flavors of *Food Trucks of the Zombie Apocalypse*?

Now you can bring a taste of Hawthorne's culinary creativity straight to your kitchen!

Sign up for *The Old Desk Post*, Delilah Cooke's weekly(ish) newsletter, and you'll receive a free copy of the ***Comfort in Catastrophe Cookbook***: a quirky collection of Hawthorne's survival-inspired recipes.

Packed with ingenuity and a hearty dose of small-town charm, this downloadable PDF features four simple-yet-unconventional recipes created for life on the edge of the apocalypse. Think: comfort food meets resourceful is-this-all-we-have cooking!

Signing up for the newsletter keeps you connected for more stories, updates, and bonus goodies while you enjoy Hawthorne's signature cooking chaos (no zombie attacks included).

Click here to sign up and claim your free recipes today!

Who is Delilah Cooke?

Delilah Cooke is the pen name for a successful genre author who decided to write cozy adventures (with a twist!) for fun. Her stories are heartfelt and entertaining, featuring quirky characters, themes of found family, and just the right amount of chaotic whimsy. As a GenX author, Delilah draws inspiration from unique snapshots in time and place that blend nostalgia, optimism, and a dash of irreverence to create worlds readers fall in love with.

Despite living in Florida, Delilah is nonetheless unapologetically queer, holding progressive values that often inform the themes of community, kindness, and resilience woven throughout her works. When not writing, she enjoys the tactile art of book binding, turning loose pages into beautiful, tangible creations—a craft that reflects her love for thoughtful, hand-crafted storytelling.

Delilah Cooke's stories invite readers to step into her playful, heartfelt universes where chaos and connection always go hand in hand.

Sign up for Delilah Cooke's Old Desk Post Newsletter!

Full Copyright

Published by Delilah Cooke

Florida | United States of America

Transformative Use Statement

Fanworks Policy

Creators are welcome to create fanworks in any format and style, but they may not share these works directly with the author. For legal and ethical reasons, Delilah Cooke cannot read, view, or watch fanworks featuring her characters. While she genuinely wishes this were possible, she must maintain these boundaries for everyone's protection. Any requests to review fanworks, or links to such works, will be immediately deleted.

Derivative Works Policy

Authors who wish to *write* and sell original stories set in worlds created by Delilah Cooke are welcome to do so, provided the works feature entirely original characters developed by the creator. However, Delilah's own characters may *not* be used as central figures in these derivative works, as this would fall under the **fanworks policy**. Limited use of her characters is permitted in the form of brief cameos (one scene only), and they may be referenced or discussed by the creator's original characters without restriction. Settings and locations from her stories are open for use and exploration.

Authors are asked to credit Delilah Cooke and provide links to her original stories, making it clear that the derivative work is set in one of her universes. Delilah Cooke is happy to promote derivative works that align with this policy.

Note that this policy does NOT extend to any audio or visual format, including but not limited to film, video, cartoons, podcasts, and comics.

www.ingramcontent.com/pod-product-compliance
Lightning Source LLC
LaVergne TN
LVHW050959080826
845145LV00009B/2362

* 9 7 8 1 9 6 8 3 0 4 0 1 0 *